Submitting to the Viking Warrior
By Lily Harlem

Chapter One

Ingrid shivered by the waning fire. Her meagre log store didn't bode well for the long winter ahead. She simply hadn't managed to summon the energy to fell and chop. But if she were frugal, 'haps there'd be enough until spring.

Spring. Just the word was lean in her mouth. It was so far away. The heavy snow, the kind that blocked the pass to Halsgrof, had only just begun to fall that morn. And now, the way it had floated a thick blanket onto the hills, stuck to the barren cliff edges, and draped the longhouse in white, Ingrid knew the only way to town would be obstructed. And as the days went on, more snow would fall, creating the giant rifts the gods blew on to create avalanches that would bury a warrior, no matter how strong and fierce he might be.

She sighed and rubbed her palms on her upper arms, trying to create warmth from the friction. This was it. She was alone now in Cativad—a place that was made up of one small farm. Hers.

She'd have to do her best to survive. If her daughter, Tove, had indeed been picked by the great King Njal to become his queen, the spring would mean a new life for her daughter. Comfort, protection, respect even. Tove would make a wonderful queen. The people of Halsgrof couldn't fail to adore her.

Ingrid's daughter was kind and gentle, yet she knew her own mind. She was brave but not foolish, and clever but not bloated with pride. King Njal could do much worse, in fact, he couldn't do better.

The wind howled through a sword-shaped gap in the rafters. Several dots of snow danced in triumphantly. Ingrid frowned. She'd fixed the roof as best she could. Luckily her husband, now feasting with the gods, had made it well all those years ago. But like the seasons, roofs didn't last forever. Indeed the barn roof was in even worse repair. Her goats and chickens would have to be herded into the longhouse when the loch froze. Not something Ingrid would enjoy.

Her small home was paltry, but she took pride in keeping it clean and making the most of the few possessions she had.

She poked at her tunic. The material was frayed, and it would benefit a wash. But this was her warmest one, to part with it for cleaning would mean a day and night of being chilly.

"Oh, my dearest Frode," she whispered. "If only you had not left me. If only it was I with you on this night and not the gods." She squeezed her eyes closed. It had been so long since her husband, Frode, had died, Tove a girl of only a few summers. It was becoming harder for Ingrid to conjure his face in her memory.

To recall his naked body against hers was even harder. He'd bedded her only a handful of times, enough, it seemed, for one daughter and naught else. Ingrid had wanted more babes, he hadn't given it, not because he didn't love her, but because that was the way the gods had decided his fate.

Frustrated, she'd taken to finding her own pleasure, in secret. Touching herself and thinking of him to rid the tension from her body in sweet pulses that rippled through her pelvis. That was one of the few things that hadn't changed when he'd died because her physical satisfaction hadn't been something he'd been involved with when he was alive.

Again the wind pressed against the longhouse. The bones of the walls creaked, and the door strained against its iron hinges.

"In the name of Thor," Ingrid muttered, standing. Snow had skittered beneath the door and was piling up against an empty barrel that had once contained Frode's mead.

Reluctantly, she left the feeble warmth of the fire and poked sacks into the gap. Her fingers were stiff and pale. "I should have gone to the town with Tove." Maybe it would have been worth leaving the livestock to fend for themselves and giving up what little she had left. The town at least held hope of work, food, and shelter. Here, hope was a thin spider-thread to cling to, the only certainty was a long, bitterly cold winter with many days of solitary darkness.

Her stomach growled, and she placed her hand over it and turned back to the fire. Her insides felt hollow, concave. She was empty of everything.

Suddenly, the door clattered loudly. Three hard bangs that almost broke the wood from the metal.

She spun to face it, her heart rate ramping up. Was that the wind?

Bang. Bang. Bang.

She gasped. No, not the wind. A bear woken by the storm and starving for food? A wolf hurling itself in desperation to get in and eat her? An elk intent on finding shelter?

"Let me in, woman?"

A man? Who? Why?

"Open this door. I tell you. Do it now." A deep, dark voice.

"Who...who are you?" Her throat was tight with fear.

"I said do it now, before the balls between my legs freeze."

Bang. Bang. Bang.

Quickly Ingrid unbolted the door and pulled it open to a flurry of snow and a blast of icy wind.

She was faced with a giant of a man, made all the taller and wider by the enormous hooded wolf pelt he had thrown over his shoulders. His beard was thick and black, and from beneath heavy eyebrows his dark, narrow eyes glared at her.

"Your barn is a disgrace," he said, pushing past her and into her home. "The roof good for naught."

"You've...you've been in my barn?" She stared at him as he stomped snow on the floor that was instantly swept up by the gusting wind to dance between them.

"Aye." He pointed at the door, his hand the size of a plate. "Shut that up, wench, it's winter if you hadn't noticed."

"I had noticed, and I'll shut it when you leave."

He huffed. "I won't be leaving. Shut the door."

"You will leave, right now, or in the name of Odin, I'll…I'll…"

"You'll what?" He shoved his hood down, sending a white powdery sprinkle into the air. "Huh? Tell me. What will you do?"

"I'll…I'll make you leave."

"I don't think so, Ingrid."

Her mouth fell open. "How do you know my name?"

"You are the mother of Tove, our queen, new wife of King Njal, am I right?"

"Oh!" She fluttered her hand over her chest. Had she heard him properly? Could her dreams for Tove have come true? Was this Viking really standing before her saying these things? Or had she gotten so cold and lonely and wrapped up in her loss for Frode and missing Tove that she'd created him out of her imagination, a wicked trick played on her by the gods?

"So? Are you?" he demanded.

"The mother of Tove, aye, aye, I am."

He grunted, stepped past her, and slammed the door. "Good, then I am where I was ordered to journey to by King Njal."

He stood close, looming over her. The scent of the mountains and snow, the sea and earth filled her nose and lungs. Had she ever felt so small? The man was a giant, a head and a half taller than her, as big as a bear.

"King Njal?"

"Aye, I was sent to please his new bride. She wouldn't see you go without, so I am here."

"Here with what?"

"Supplies."

"Er…" She stepped back and spread her palms. "Where are my supplies? I don't see them."

"In your barn, yonder." He gestured to the door. "We will unload the wagon after I have filled my belly and slept." He walked to the fire, shrugging out of his cloak and then tossing it on a bench.

She rushed after him. "We should do it now? The barn is—"

"In a state of such disrepair your husband should be ashamed to be a Viking."

"My husband..." She tilted her chin. "Was a fine Viking."

"Was?"

"Now he feasts with Odin and Thor, Frigg and Loki. He raises his drink to those who are yet to join him. Including you..." She raised her eyebrows.

"Ah yes, me, I am Gunnar of Barosvik." He banged his hand on his chest, shifting a brooch in the image of a snake's head. "Son of Ifor of Barosvik." He paused. "And I am sorry for your loss. And for the queen's loss of a father."

She stared at him for a moment, searching for sincerity. It was in his voice, but was it in his eyes?

Before she could see, he sat at the table, the stool legs scraping on the floor. "So feed me, wench, a feast. I have traveled far on this evil night. And mead, pour me mead."

"Feed you? Mead?" She gestured to a shelf that held a basket of dried fish, a bag of grain, and several jars of preserved fruit and cabbage. "You really think I can prepare you a feast out of that?"

"That is your supply?" His eyes widened.

For a moment shame washed over her, but she had no room for that emotion, it could take a hike into the wilderness. This was reality, *her* reality. Life had been hard. She'd saved Tove by sending her away, but herself... perhaps she hadn't wanted saving. Maybe joining Frode and the gods had been a plan Ingrid had hatched yet refused to acknowledge.

"What in the name of the All Father were you going to eat this winter? The loch will be frozen as hard as a stone in your boot before you know it, woman? And the hills here are harsh, the land poor." He shook his head. "Was not a good place to set up a homestead and raise a daughter."

"It was where we landed," Ingrid said. "When we came from our wedding in a fjord north of here."

"Would not have been my choice." He shook his head then reached for his cloak. "Put another log on the fire and water on to heat."

"But I don't have many..."

"You have logs now I am here with my axe." His beard twitched, as though he'd set his jaw tight. "So use what you have freely." He swung his cloak back on, the movement sending a breeze through the air. "Logs are no longer a problem."

"Where are you going?"

"To the cart, to get us food. I had not anticipated you living with so little."

He turned and stomped to the door.

Ingrid stared after him. Just a few heartbeats previously she'd resigned herself to a cold, hungry night, yet now this warrior had appeared, gruff, demanding, and enormous, but with food and the promise of fuel.

She threw a log in her fire trough and stoked the ashes to bring flames back to life. She then scooped several ladles of barreled water into the cauldron atop it. When she'd done that, she rushed to the door and pulled it open to the milky darkness.

She gritted her teeth and narrowed her eyes. The cold was painful and the wind spiteful. Through the flurry, she made out Gunnar entering the barn; his big boots had dug deep indents in his wake.

Her goats and hens would bleat and squawk when a stranger walked in, she knew that. But he'd already put a cart in there, likely a horse or two as well, so she wouldn't rush to calm them.

She glanced left, toward the fjord. It was only just visible through the sideways-blowing snow, but already a white sheen had landed on it—it wouldn't be long before ice claimed the surface and stayed there for many moons.

Tomorrow, she'd drag Frode's boat onto the pebbled bank. It was barely worth saving, but she wasn't about to willingly destroy something that had been his.

A noise to her right.

Gunnar was trudging back from the barn, his shoulders swinging and the squall catching his long dark hair. He held a sack under one arm and a small barrel in the other.

When he reached the door, she stepped aside to let him in, then quickly shut it. "What do you have?"

He didn't reply. Instead, he set the barrel atop Frode's empty one, pulled a horn from the sack, and filled it with mead. He drank deep, his gulps noisy and his eyes closed.

"Ah, that is better." He wiped the back of his hand over his mouth. "Get yerself a horn and I'll fill it for you."

Ingrid did as he'd instructed.

"And this, for you." He took the horn, and in its place presented a red garment.

"What is it?"

"A gift from King Njal and the queen. It is all from them. Many gifts."

"And the mead? The mead you're drinking is mine?"

He paused, then. "I'm sure you would not deny a warrior who risked his life to bring these gifts a drink and a meal."

"No, of course not." That hadn't been what she'd meant. Her brain was still catching up with the fact that her daughter was the new queen and that she had renewed supplies. "Please, sup all you want."

He inclined his head as a gesture of appreciation.

"And this." She unfolded the material. "It is beautiful." Made of thick wool, the blood-red cloak had glinting golden thread along the seams and a hood of the softest wolf fur she'd ever felt.

"Aye, it will keep you warm until I can fix this roof." He gestured upward.

"You'll do that?"

"Aye, it has to be done." He handed her a drink.

Before she took it, she draped the cloak over her shoulders. It was heavy and instantly trapped heat against her body. "I thank you."

He didn't reply. He refilled his drink then began plucking items from the sack and placing them on the table beside the fire.

Dried fish wrapped in linen, a loaf of rye bread, a jug of buttermilk, and pots of honey, pickled greens, and roasted hazelnuts.

Ingrid's eyes grew wide, and her stomach clenched. "There is so much."

"It will fill our bellies this eve." He set the sack aside and picked up the bread. He tore a chunk and bit into it. "Tomorrow we will stack and sort the rest of the supplies to ensure the mice don't get it."

"There's more?" She watched his beard twitch as he chewed.

"Aye, enough to last all winter, enough to last both of us all winter."

Chapter Two

What? Had she heard him right? Both of them? For the winter? All winter? "But...what...I mean..." she stuttered.

He sat beside the fire, his frame huge on her small chair, and continued to eat the bread. A sprinkle of crumbs caught on his leather tunic that was held at the waist by a wide brass buckled belt.

"You can't...Gunnar of Barosvik, you can't stay here all winter."

"So where do you propose I stay?" He tipped his head, his brow a slash of frown lines. "In the barn?"

"No." She gestured in the direction of Halsgrof. "You can go back to the town."

He huffed. "How can I do that?" He snatched up a fish and bit into it.

"The way you came..." Her heart sank as she realized the problem. "And now, go this moment, before the pass is blocked with snow."

"You want me to leave now, wench?"

"Aye. Right now." She rushed up to him and gripped his upper arm. Tugged. "Move."

He didn't budge.

"Come on, quickly, this snow will block the pass. You know it will." Still she pulled at him.

"I am not moving from where I sit, woman." He shrugged as if she were no more than an annoying insect.

"You must, you must go now. It is the only way." She pulled him harder. Putting all of her muscle and effort into it and heaving.

"It is not for you to say." He curled his big fingers around her forearm and stilled her. "It is not your decision, mother of the queen."

"Ingrid. My name is Ingrid, and this is my house. It is my decision, and yes, I am the mother of the queen, don't forget that."

"That may be so as of today, and it may be your home, but without your husband, that makes me the man of this longhouse. The Viking whose word is heard and obeyed beneath this roof." He scowled at the gap in the roof. "Now leave me be. I am tired and hungry after my journey."

She stepped back and glared at him. He was as stubborn as he was big. As immovable as the mountain yonder. "You will leave tomorrow." She slammed her hands onto her hips. "I am telling you that as I stand here before the gods."

He drank from his horn and rested back farther. "Eat, woman, before your bones break through your skin."

Ingrid resisted the urge to swipe at him, to stamp her foot in anger or pick up the poker and strike his head. The truth was, food was calling her. Its voice loud to her stomach and competing with her frustration that this warrior had settled into her longhouse with the intention of staying.

She reached for a wooden bowl, blew out several dust motes, and placed a fish, hazelnuts, and pickles into it. She also grabbed some bread before Gunnar ate it all.

Sitting opposite him, with the fire trough between, she started to eat. The fish was smoky and fleshy, the hazelnuts fresh and sweet. And the bread, it had been baked by someone with skill, likely the baker to the king and queen.

"Good, aye?" Gunnar asked with a mouthful of food.

"It's good." She sipped her drink.

He leaned forward and added another log.

She opened her mouth to object, they were precious, but then remembered what he'd said about chopping more.

When the pass was closed, the forest stretched all around for two days' walking, there was no shortage of trees, she'd just had a shortage of strength.

She helped herself to another fish. Perhaps if she'd eaten like this in the weeks before the snows came, she'd have swung an axe with the force of Thor.

The water in the cauldron bubbled, steam dancing upward.

Gunnar moved it to one side then filled his palm with nuts.

"So tell me," Ingrid said. "Were there many brides for King Njal to choose from?"

"No, just a handful. Though one was Princess Hilda of Kaldaross."

"Oh."

"She is very beautiful."

"So why did the king not choose her?"

"The king is a wise man." He paused. "Beauty can be a mask hiding an ugly face beneath."

"Did something happen?" Ingrid wished she'd been there.

"Let's just say he saw beneath the mask." Gunnar threw a nut into the air, tipped his head back, and caught it in his mouth. He chewed, grinned. "You should be pleased, he liked everything he saw when he looked at your Tove, our new queen."

"She is a beautiful person inside and out." Ingrid tipped her chin. "Frode and I taught her to be kind and generous as well as a strong, brave maiden."

"Which is what the king saw." He swiped his palms together, the nuts finished. "As well, of course, as a woman fit for bedding and child-rearing."

Ingrid nodded. She hoped Tove wouldn't find her first night as a wife too traumatic and that the goddess, Freya, would be with her.

Frode had been gentle with his bride, or as gentle as Ingrid believed a Viking could be. But would King Njal be the same? He was a ruler, a warrior, and a brave explorer. Would he be dominant and demanding and seek only his own pleasure? Or would Tove's pale skin and delicate frame bring out the gentle side in him? Soften him into touching her with a feathery caress and a honey sweet embrace?

"And talking of bedding," Gunnar said. "It is that time."

"Bedding?" She held the bread aloft between plate and mouth. "What do you—?"

"Not that." He frowned. "My bones are weary, the journey was long and cold. I need to sleep." He stood. "You have a big bed."

He was right. She did. It was made of fine oak and had carvings of dragons on the headboard. The mattress was straw and lined with animal skins. Pulled up close to the fire trough for warmth, it was where Ingrid spent her time during the darkest of winter days.

"It will do." He stepped past her, unbuckling his belt. He dropped it to the floor, then leaned over the hot water and splashed his face. He didn't dry it, just let the water cling to his beard and drip from the end of his nose as he walked to the bed.

"But I—"

He dropped onto the bed the way a rock would into a puddle, landing facedown, arms either side. He groaned then sighed, sagging as though his exhalation was deflating him.

Ingrid glared at him. He had the nerve of a fox at a chicken coop. That was her bed. Where was she to sleep?

He moaned again, and then a loud, rattling snore emerged. Another followed, then another.

She rolled her eyes. "My gods, what are you doing to me?"

Setting her bowl aside, she finished her drink then clasped her new cloak beneath her chin. Her blood was warming, finally, and she could no longer see her breath floating in the air when she breathed out. Her stomach was full, the ache of emptiness alleviated.

Gunnar of Barosvik's arrival had been welcome. She wouldn't deny that. But his departure would also be welcome. This was not his home and that was not his bed. Once he'd unpacked the supplies and chopped some wood, he could make his way to the pass and get through before it was well and truly sealed with snow.

First thing tomorrow.

Ingrid woke to the sharp crack of axe splitting wood.

Her neck also felt like wood. She'd slept awkwardly on the bench with her back to the wall.

With a grimace, she stood and encouraged the fire back to life with another log.

A shard of light pierced the roof, and she knew she'd slept for many hours. Without the discomfort of an empty stomach, and the warmth of the new cloak, she'd drifted through a deep and dreamless night.

Crack. Crack. Crack.

The bed was empty. Gunnar clearly up and chopping fuel.

"Good, he can do that, then get out of here, off my land." She poured a bowl of buttermilk and drank. It tasted delicious, and she hoped there was more.

She was excited to sort through her new supplies, but she would do that once Gunnar left. As long as everything Tove and the king had sent was off the cart he could go, she'd do the rest. And if he replenished her log store beforehand, well, she'd put in a good word about him when she met her new son in the spring.

New son. The king. Tove a queen.

Pushing her hair over her shoulders, she stepped outside, her heart swelling with pride. She was going places. She'd be the grandmother of future kings and queens. Who could have guessed the gods would weave such a rich path for her?

Snow was still falling but with no rush to get to its destination on the earth. Flakes twirled on the breeze as if making the most of being free, dancing upward and sideways and taking in the view.

She followed Gunnar's footprints to the opposite side of the barn, snowflakes sticking to her new cloak and dampening her cheeks. Still the axe continued to land on wood. A rhythmic *thud-thud* that reminded her of Frode.

But of course it wasn't Frode standing at the block, it was Gunnar.

With the axe held aloft, his naked torso was stretched, highlighting the roped muscles in his arms and shoulders and the ridges of strength in his belly. His leather pants sat low on his hips, a trail of dark hair drifting from his sternum to the waistband. His skin wasn't pale, it was the color of a hazelnut, except for a raised pale-pink scar on his chest, a wedge shape, as though someone had taken a slice from him.

Again he brought the axe down. The wood halved and flew to the ground. He stooped, picked up another chunk ready for chopping. His brow was shiny with sweat, as was the hair of his underarms.

"Thank you," she said. "For chopping wood."

"We'll need it." He raised the axe, gritted his teeth, slammed it down.

"*I* will need it."

He paused, frowned. His beard was peppered with tiny snowflakes. "I said we because I will winter with you."

"No, no, that is not going to happen." The very thought squeezed her heart. She couldn't share her home with a big brute like him. That was out of the question. She wanted to be alone with her animals and her supplies and in the spring make the journey to Halsgrof.

"It is not for you to decide." He wiped his brow on the back of his arm.

"It most certainly is."

"It is up to the gods." He pointed upward. "They have—"

"And I'll tell you something else." She pointed at him. "I will be telling the king how you just stomped into my home and acted as if you were entitled to it." Her voice was rising. Her damp cheeks were flushing.

"Tell the king?" He nodded slowly then picked up another chunk of wood. "I cannot say that makes me fearful, wench."

"Well, it should, I'll have his ear. And Tove, my daughter, already does."

He cracked the wood in half, his powerful body solid at the moment of impact.

"So get your things." She gestured to his clothing, discarded on a log. "And leave before the pass is blocked with snow."

"The pass is already blocked with snow."

"It won't be. It's barely snowing right now."

"I only just made it through yesterday, you were nearly left here alone to die, Ingrid."

"That is not true. The pass will still be clear." In truth, Ingrid wasn't sure, but she wouldn't be happy until Gunnar had at least tried to get through it.

"It is truth." He began stacking the logs beside the barn. "You are stuck with me for this winter."

"No. No." Anger swarmed in her veins. "That is not the truth. I cannot have you here."

"Why not?" He held out his palms. "I am useful. Look at these hands, they can do many things."

"They can also set to the task of putting a saddle on your horse and leaving." She pulled open the creaking door to the barn. "They can do that, your hands."

The chickens squawked, the goats bleated, and a magnificent bay horse rose its head from a pile of her precious hay.

"Now. Go. While there is light." She pointed at the sun's weak circlet behind the clouds. "I am ordering you."

"You're ordering me." He folded his arms, his knuckles pressing on his bulging biceps.

"Aye, know your place, Viking."

His right eyebrow twitched, as did his beard.

She half huffed, half grunted, her frustration growing by the second. Why was he still standing there, half naked and ignoring the bitter cold? Her scalp itched with annoyance, and her cloak was suddenly suffocating.

"Know my place," he repeated, the muscles between his neck and shoulders tensing. Two sharp triangles of power.

"Your horse is fed and rested," she said, stepping into the barn. "Time for you to go, I...oh!"

He'd swooped up behind her and wrapped his arms around her waist. His grip was as strong as any bear as he hoisted her into air, slamming her back against his bare chest.

"Get off me!" she yelled.

"Stop telling me what to do, woman." He kicked the barn door closed with a bang, much to the shock of the chickens and goats. "I will not tolerate it."

"It is your place... for me to tell... you what to do."

"That is where you are wrong. I am a Viking warrior. We are alone here..." He marched toward the chopping block, a thick old stump the height of a chair. "We are alone here for the winter, and that is something that will not surprise either the king or the queen as they sent me off when the winter snow was falling."

She wriggled against him and tried to peel his arms from her waist. It was no good. His hold was sound and tight. "Put me down."

"As you wish."

Suddenly she was on the floor but only upright for a second because then the snowy world turned upside down as she was folded in half, over his bent knee.

She yelped in indignation and her hood skimmed the dust and her belly squashed onto his thigh. "Stop this!" she cried.

"Cry out all you want, there's naught here to hear you but animals."

Ingrid pushed and tried to stand. It was no good. His left leg had trapped her there. "You have no right...let me go."

"It's obvious, Ingrid, that you have been without a Viking man in your life for too long. You have become insolent, ungrateful, and disrespectful."

He shoved at her new cloak. It flipped over her head, surrounding her, brushing the floor and wrapping her in red glow. She gripped his pants and continued to try and wriggle free.

"Keep still. I will teach you to control your mouth and accept our fate." He pushed the center of her back, tipping her farther. "And I will teach you that lesson now."

"Oh, Freya and all the gods in Valhalla, save me." Her behind was now the highest point of her body, and she was well and truly imprisoned by his hold on her. She was trapped and vulnerable, at his mercy.

"Without a man to put you over his knee, it's clear you have lost your ability to obey." Gunnar yanked at her frayed tunic. "But we will soon fix that."

"I'll speak to my daughter about this, and she will have your—"

Slap.

"Oh!" She jerked forward as a heated spank landed over her cheeks, his big hand sending pain and heat sparking through her clothing onto her flesh.

Slap.

She gasped. "How dare you. Get off me."

"Next time you tell me to know my place." He rubbed over her pants, the only barrier between his hand and her bare bottom. "You will think twice."

He didn't give her time to answer, he spanked her again, then again.

She squealed and cursed and gasped with each hard strike. White-hot burn was streaking over her flesh. Her bottom heating in a way it never had before. Frodo hadn't spanked her. He never would have, it was not the way of his soul.

She squeezed her eyes closed as Gunnar's punishment continued, tears dampening her eyelashes. It wasn't just the pain, it was the indignation. How dare he? How dare he treat her this way? She wasn't his to punish, she wasn't his to be in charge of.

He paused with his hand resting on her behind as though he did own it.

She kicked up her heels, catching his leg with the right one. "You cannot do this, you cannot..."

"I am and I can." He swiped her butt again, swift and sharp.

"Ouch!"

"I will not allow you to behave this way," he said. "I have brought you supplies to ensure your survival this winter. I am chopping wood to keep us warm. I will fix your broken roof and another hundred things that require the attention of a man." He paused; he was breathing fast. "So you will be grateful, you will be glad that I am here, and you will obey me, wench."

Obey him!

She pinched his leg through his pants. Hard.

"Stop that. You are making this worse for yourself."

Spank. Spank. Spank.

Again the thwacks rained down. She wasn't cold now, she was hot—hot and angry and mortified. This stranger had taken his hand to her rump as if he were her husband.

Which he most definitely was not and never would be.

Just when she thought her bottom would burst into flames, he stopped.

Her breaths were coming in short throaty sobs and warming the air trapped by the cloak over her head. Her heart was pounding, and her pulse loud in her ears.

"Let me be." Again she pushed at his legs.

This time he allowed her to lift. He pulled her until she was perched on his lap.

Her head swam, and little black dots danced in her vision. She swayed.

"I've got you." He tightened an arm around her waist.

The action enraged her more.

"Get off me." She stood, staggered, and clutched the edge of the barn. "You have no right...to do...that."

He rubbed his palms together and tipped his head. "Do you need more?"

"No!"

"Then I suggest you stop telling me what I can and can't do, Ingrid. Now I am here, I am responsible for you, the queen's mother, the livestock, and this home. It is on my shoulders to ensure we all survive this land's harsh winter."

"But—"

"Ah." He held up one finger and stood. "It would serve you well to hold your words in. The gods blessed me with imagination when it comes to doling out punishments for insolence and disagreeing."

She stared at him, open-mouthed. She wanted to slap away the conceited grin that had twisted his lips.

But she knew doing that would get her over his lap again, or judging by what he'd just said, worse.

She flicked her hood up and smoothed the front of her cape. Her bottom was smarting, her skin still hot. Without saying a word, she spun around and stomped through the snow to the longhouse.

Did the gods think it amusing to place her with Gunnar of Barosvik for the long, dark months ahead? Perhaps that was what entertained them. In which case she'd make a sacrifice, one of the chickens, and then maybe he'd befall an accident or run into a hungry wolf pack.

Yes, that would suit her very well.

Chapter Three

Ingrid stared at her overflowing shelves. Never had she been so well-stocked. Tove and King Njal had been generous, and there was plenty of food for the winter for her and the animals. And if Gunnar saw fit to hunt, too, they certainly wouldn't be hungry.

She rubbed her sore bottom. Perhaps she'd even put some meat on her bones. It had been a long time since she'd had her own layer of protection from the cold nights.

Turning at a sound on the roof, she glanced upward.

Gunnar was up there, on the outside, banging. It was dark, but he'd announced there was more chance of him growing breasts than sleeping with snow blowing toward the bed again. He'd scrambled up there, hammer in hand.

Ingrid didn't complain. It would be good to have the roof fixed.

She unfolded several new blankets and examined the weave. They were intricate and skillfully made. She'd give her threadbare ones to the animals and have new for herself.

When she'd spread two blankets on the bed, she tossed another log onto the fire. Sparks flew upward, and she smiled and held her hands out for the warmth. It was the first time the log store had been full since Frode had died. Gunnar had chopped wood over and over, from sunup until sundown. His arms working the way she imagined a god's would, tireless and powerful.

She was grateful, really she was. But that didn't stop her wishing he'd leave.

"Woman!"

"Aye?" She stared upward.

"Make me food. Heat water." His growling voice was muffled and caught on the growling wind. "You hear me?"

"Aye, I hear you." She clicked her tongue on the roof of her mouth. If he was going to treat her like a slave, she'd find some herbs to make him sick, teach *him* a lesson.

He started banging again.

Ingrid placed a cauldron of water over the fire to heat. She then put bread on the table along with cabbage, dried wild greens, and smoked fowl.

Sipping buttermilk, she then sat on the bench, softer now she'd covered it with a new flame-red fox fur.

Gunnar was descending, his bulk shaking the timbers. He landed with a soft *whump* on the other side of the wall she sat against.

"Ah, good," he said a few minutes later as he strode in, slamming the door behind himself and then throwing his cloak to one side. "My stomach is as empty as a mead barrel after a great feast." He popped a chunk of fowl into his mouth and chewed. "Yer roof is fixed. Don't know how you lived with it like that for so long."

"I was going to fix it up."

He didn't answer, just raised one eyebrow and reached for his horn. He filled it with mead and drank.

"The new chickens have settled in," she said. "The others have stopped pecking them. I'd wager there'll be eggs 'morrow."

"A bit of grain and they forget to be peckers." He stuck his finger in the warming water. "Ah good. When I have eaten I will bathe."

She glanced at the old wooden tub in the corner. Like the roof, it had sprung a leak. "You will?"

"Aye." He sat at the table and started on the food.

Ingrid nibbled fowl and greens and drained her buttermilk.

When Gunnar had finished, he wrapped his hand around his wiry beard, tugged it, and frowned.

"What is it?" she asked.

"This." His mouth downturned. "It has to go."

"But it will keep you warm."

"I will grow another in time." He nodded at her. "Besides, you don't have one, and your chin doesn't turn black and fall off in the winter."

She touched her face and laughed despite her lingering irritation with him. "I hope not."

He stood, the chair legs scraping. "Now where is it?"

For a moment he rummaged in his sack and then produced a block of chestnut soap wrapped in linen and a sharp blade with a white-boned handle.

Then he sat at the table, a wooden bowl of water in front of him, and hacked at his beard.

Ingrid watched on, curious. Frode had trimmed and adorned his beard with beads on occasion, but he had never removed it entirely.

When Gunnar had trimmed his beard short, he soaped his hands until they were fluffy with suds and soaked his beard. He then carefully, slowly, and repeatedly rinsed the blade and scraped away at the stubble.

Soon his jawline was smooth and the angles sharp. A silvery jagged scar on his chin was evident.

"Mmm," he said, almost to himself as he rubbed his palm around his face. "Haven't felt that for a while." He looked at her. "Now for the head."

"Your head?"

"Aye."

She stood. "No, you really will be cold."

"It is good to take if off and—"

"Not this time of year." She took the blade. "But if you insist let me try something."

His eyebrows rose. "What do you have in your mind?"

"I will take some off, not all, tidy it the way my mother did my father's."

"No, I want it all off." He grabbed a handful and tugged hard.

"And freeze your scalp?" She put her hand on her hip, cocked it to the left, and frowned. "And whatever brain you have in there."

He shrugged, a smile tugging his mouth. "Go on then. If I don't like it, I'll shave it anyway."

"You will like it." She dipped her hands into the warm water and found the soap. "Trust me."

"Trust has to be earned." He let out a gruff, throaty sound.

"Some would say it is there until lost." She stepped behind him and lathered his hair.

"Did your husband trust you?"

"Aye, of course. I had never done anything to lose his trust."

"You always pleased him?"

She paused, then, "I did my duties as a wife, here, on the farm."

"And that included following his word, his every instruction?"

"I gave him a daughter." She thinned his hair around his right ear. She would shave three inches above each ear, from temple to nape. The top she would plait tight to his scalp.

"You are avoiding my question."

"I do not understand what you are asking, Gunnar."

"I will resay my words. I am telling you that no matter how obedient or disobedient you were with your husband, that is of no consequence to how it is now I am here."

"And tell me, how is it now?" She held the tip of his ear out of the way and ran the blade against his skin, creating a small scraping sound.

"I wish to be very clear. I am the warrior Viking in this longhouse, and you are a small maiden. It is obvious you have been too long without a man, the farm is in disrepair, and you were woefully ill prepared for winter."

Her jaw clenched as she rinsed the blade.

"If I had not arrived at the insistence of the king and queen, you would have not survived, so as such you will obey me, you will do as I tell you without question. This is how it will be. I am your master, and you will be grateful for all that I do here."

"Is that right?" Her cheeks flared, and it had nothing to do with the fact she was standing beside the fire.

"Yes, that is right. And you *will* understand."

She continued to remove his thick hair, revealing a scalp that was rich with fading blue ink. Swirling shapes that looped in circles through each other, some ending in points like spears.

"It will be a long winter," he went on after a while. "A long winter alone, the two of us."

"And not one I am relishing."

"I agree the nights will be black, cold, and quiet. We will have no company except animals."

Ingrid was silent. What was he getting at?

"You should know I am a man with needs." His voice was low and dark, seeming to grate from his throat. "The same as your husband was."

For the love of Freya. He's talking about sex. His need for sex.

She opened her mouth to confess Frode had barely touched her but closed it again. That was not information for Gunnar to have. "Your needs are of no concern to me." She started on the opposite side of his head.

"They're not?"

"No." She scraped at his hair a little rougher than before. "They are not."

"Ah..."

"What does 'ah' mean?"

"It means that, ah, we will see, woman, just how much my needs will concern you."

His needs...concern me?

A small flame lit low in her belly. It traveled between her legs, and she clamped her thighs together, holding it there. She had no idea what it would be like to lie with a warrior like Gunnar, to have his big cock fill her. Likely she wouldn't be able to take him after all this time without a man.

But the thought of it brought her cunny to life. A pleasant buzz of anticipation that tensed the muscles deep inside.

"Have you nearly finished, woman?" He shifted on the seat.

"Aye, hold still or I will draw blood."

He huffed and folded his arms. "I could have shaved it all off by now."

"You will like this." She pushed thoughts of his needs aside. "And thank me for it."

He didn't answer, and she pursed her lips and finished shaving the right side of his head. She then started on the hair atop his head, weaving it around her fingers and pulling it into an intricate plait ensuring no strand was missed.

The fire crackled, and he stared at it as though mesmerized by the flicking flames tickling the base of the cauldron as it steamed. His wide shoulders were unmoving, his breaths shallow. Ingrid couldn't help but think of him as a sleeping dragon, one who appeared peaceful but could spring into powerful action at any moment. Instantly become a warrior ready to fight and kill, an explorer ready for high waves and danger, or a man prepared to tip a woman over his knee for a sound spanking.

The memory of that made her bottom cheeks tingle, and a new rush of humiliation gripped her chest.

She reached the end of the plait and collected a needle and thread. As she sewed it secure, she had to resist the temptation to spike him with the needle as payment for the spanking.

But she did resist. His skin was so thick he probably wouldn't feel it anyway.

"I have finished."

He stood, his hands coming to his head to feel the new style. "It is neat and tight."

"Aye, that is how my father wore his. It will keep your head warmer than if you shaved it all off but will require little attention."

"Mmm." He nodded, his lips a tight line that did hold a hint of approval.

Ingrid twisted her fingers together and studied him. Without the huge ragged beard and messy hair, Gunnar was a handsome man. Battle-scarred, aye, but his features were strong and symmetrical, his eyes intelligent and his ears neither too big nor too small. Ingrid always had noticed ears. "So you like it?"

"You did well." He nodded, the reflection of the flames catching in his eyes. "Now I will bathe."

He peeled off his hairy tunic, tossing it aside, and stomped to the tub. He carried it to the fire and set it down. "What is this?" He sighed and shook his head at the crack. "Like everything else in this farmstead, it is broken."

"I have been meaning to fix it, here." She rushed to the new box of long, slim candles. "It is a small crack, fill it with wax."

"Ingrid." He took the candle, studying her face. "That is again a good idea of yours. I would have set about it another way which would have been time-consuming when I am in need of a bath."

Her stomach clenched, and a strange, unfamiliar rush of pleasure went through her veins. She had impressed him. Something she got the feeling wasn't easy to do with Gunnar.

He took the candle, his fingertips brushing hers, and set about filling the small crack with wax.

While he molded it, she checked the water and reached for her supply of soap that was infused with lavender from the meadow yonder. It was one of Tove's favorite scents.

"That should keep the water in." He stood. "I will fill it now."

Ingrid stepped aside and he hoisted the large cauldron into the air by its handle then tipped it into the tub. The muscles in his arms, shoulders, and back stood proud, pushing against his tanned skin.

When he'd put both cauldrons of steaming water into the tub, he examined the repaired patch. "I fear it will leak a bit, but it will give me time to bathe." He looked at her. "Fill the cauldrons again. More hot water will be needed."

Ingrid picked them up then went to the barrel she kept her water supply in. She filled them, the water gushing, then turned.

Her heart skipped a beat then did an extra two to catch up.

Gunnar was standing naked beside the tub.

If his face was handsome without his beard, then his body was utterly beautiful without clothes. If ever a god came to earth as a Norseman, he'd surely come in the image of Gunnar.

His long legs were thick and strong. His left thigh held the same swirling ink as that on his scalp. His belly was bricked with muscle, and a dense trail of hair led to his cock.

His cock.

Not erect, but also not flaccid, was bigger than Ingrid believed a cock could be.

Her breath stuttered, and a quiver attacked her cunny as he stepped into the steaming water.

His buttocks were taut. The right held a scar that went to the base of his spine in an arc, as though a sword had caught him when he'd been turned.

"Aye, this is good," he said on a sigh and sank deep.

Ingrid swallowed and pushed aside a little voice in her head that told her not to admire this naked Viking who wasn't her husband.

But she didn't need nor want to hear that voice. For so long she'd lived untouched, unpleasured. So what harm could it do to admire?

And Gunnar of Barosvik was definitely worth admiring.

Chapter Four

Gunnar splashed water on his face. "Put more water on the fire, woman."

She found herself obeying and setting the heavy cauldrons on to heat. She added two more logs, a luxury, then poured herself a horn of mead.

"Aye, I'll have one of them." He nodded at the barrel.

Again she did as he'd bid and handed him a drink.

"Thanks to you," he said, taking it and smiling. A smile that went to his eyes, small creases forming around the outer edges.

She said nothing. She was concentrating on not looking at his cock beneath the water.

"You should strip out of those old clothes," he said.

"I will do no such thing." She pressed her palm against her tatty tunic.

"They are good for naught but the animals." He frowned. "And Queen Tove has sent you new clothes. It is not fit for you, the mother of the queen, to be dressed in rags."

Rags.

Aye, he was right. They were rags. Dirty ones at that.

"When I have finished bathing." He took a drink. "You will also bathe, and I will dispose of those old clothes."

"I wish to keep them."

"I wish you not to." His gaze slid down her body, to her toes and back up to her face. "And you are being stubborn by arguing with me. You have proven you are not a stupid woman, Ingrid, do not act as such."

"Wishing to keep these clothes is not stupid."

"You know it is." He closed his eyes and rested his head back, let out a sigh. "Even if you won't admit it to me."

Steam swirled around his shoulders and face, and the scent of soap infused the air.

Ingrid nibbled on her bottom lip. The man was maddening and right. Her clothes were good for nothing but the goats to nibble on. But she wouldn't admit that, not now. He was too fond of being right, it was annoying.

She found her eyeline drifting. His cock shimmered beneath the surface of the dark soapy water, the end wide, the shaft thick.

Another strange quiver attacked her cunny, and the sweet spot between her legs trembled. It was a strange mix of want and fear. She felt like a virgin again, a scared bride.

He's going to want to bed me. Put that big thing inside me.

Ingrid knew that as sure as she knew the gods' emerald lights would stroke the sky like ribbons. She'd known enough Viking men, heard stories growing up, to know that it was a desire within them that couldn't be ignored once they'd acknowledged it.

Which Frode never really had.

"You like what you see?"

She gasped. He was staring right at her with that amused tilt to his lips once again in place.

Quickly she turned away, reached for the poker, and prodded the fire.

He chuckled. "You have been a long time without a man in your bed."

She didn't answer.

"You should know it has also been a long time for me. I have been traveling for many months, and my time at Halsgrof was short. King Njal sent for me within hours of my arrival from a journey west."

"That is of no interest to me." She sat and folded her arms. "But..."

"Speak what is on yer mind, wench."

"But what was it like? West?"

"They have good land, fine, fertile land. I traveled with King Njal's brother's fleet, though we were separated, and I do not yet know if he has returned."

"And this land, it is farmed?"

"Aye, well farmed, they are skilled, they have tools. But what they have the most of…" He rubbed the soap along his left arm.

"What? What do they have the most of?"

"Sun. Their winters are not like ours. Their days do not turn to night, even in the depths of the coldest season. Their seas and lochs do not ice, and their animals do not perish if not barned."

"That is…that is unbelievable."

"You should believe it. I have seen it with my own eyes."

"And what will King Njal do about it? What will the other kings and earls of our land do with this new knowledge?"

"They will invade, of course." He switched arms. "Take land as their own and farm it."

"Will the people of these western lands and isles allow such a thing?"

"That is of no consequence. We are bigger, stronger, more skilled when it comes to attacking and fighting."

"They are small people?"

He laughed and appeared to give his cock a good soaping. "Aye, small compared to us."

Ingrid thought for a moment. "I should like to travel one day."

"Aye, it is good for the eyes to see new things." He placed the soap on the side of the tub. "But it is also good to have a home." He stood, water sluicing down his big hard body, flowing into all the dinks and dents in shiny rivulets.

Ingrid felt as though her eyes had locked on to his wet skin, but after a moment, she tore her attention away.

This time he didn't seem to notice and swiped up a blanket. He rubbed his body roughly then secured it around his waist. "Now you will bathe?"

"I will...what?"

"Bathe." He nodded at the water. "I will remove this, you can add more from the cauldron."

"I have no intention of bathing here, now...with..."

"With what?" He frowned.

"With you here. I will bathe when you leave."

He pulled a face, his mouth downturning. "Then that will be spring, and if you want the truth, as the gods see it, you need to bathe and rid yerself of those rags."

"How dare you, I—"

"You need the truth, Ingrid. You are dressed like a homeless wanderer and your skin in need of a scrub."

She pouted and folded her arms. The scent of the soap drifted toward her again. It had become unfamiliar. 'Haps Gunnar was right. She did need to bathe. Trouble was, the filling of the old leaky tub was such a chore she'd let it slide.

But it seemed not anymore. Gunnar had filled a pail with used water and was marching to the door, the blanket wrapped low on his waist flapping. He opened the door to the snow and gale and threw the water out into the darkness.

He then repeated the action, long strides covering the ground quickly. After two more pails had been discarded, he nodded at the fresh water in the cauldron. "While I add that, in the name of Thor, woman, strip out of those flea-bitten clothes."

"There are no fleas!"

He raised his eyebrows. "Do I have to rip them from you?"

"No. Don't you even think about—"

"So strip!" he roared.

She jumped within her skin at his loud voice and harsh tone, then quickly tugged up the base of her tunic. With it removed, she stood in pants and an undergarment that covered her breasts.

"We will bathe every third day throughout this winter, it is healthy to be that way and the way of the gods. And I will not discuss it further with you."

Gunnar tipped the cauldrons into the tub, and steam quivered into the air.

She pulled off her boots, her socks, and pants. Her undergarment came down to her thighs, and with it still on, she walked up to the tub.

He stuck his hand into the water and waggled his fingers. "It is good. Get in."

She clenched her teeth and braced for the indignity of him seeing her naked.

But instead of watching her, he scooped up her discarded clothes and strode from the longhouse out into the night.

She stared at the spot he'd just been standing in. Was the man crazy? Wandering around outside in naught but a blanket and his skin still shimmering with bathing water.

Quickly, she shed the last of her clothing and slipped into the tub.

She sighed. "Oh, Freya, Loki, and Odin, this is good." The water slid around her legs, between her thighs, over her buttocks, and then up her torso. A delicious circle of heat enclosed her. She rested back, the water enveloping her breasts and making her nipples tingle. Closing her eyes, she let a wonderful shimmy of pleasure caress her skin.

"It is good, aye?"

"Oh." She opened her eyes and instinctively drew her knees up, shielding the juncture of her legs.

Gunnar stood before her, holding out a new pat of soap. Flecks of snow doused the plait running over the top of his head.

"Er, yes, it's good." She took the soap. "Thank you."

He kind of huffed then retrieved her old undergarment and threw it toward the now closed door. "There are new clothes for you to wear. Befitting of a queen's mother."

She didn't answer. Instead, she set about cleaning the ingrained dirt from her fingers. The chestnut and lavender suds were efficient, and she moved onto cleansing her body.

And then a splash of warm water streaked over her crown and down her face, blurring her vision. "What...oh!"

"Keep still, woman, your hair needs washing."

Gunnar had emptied a jug over her head, soaking through to her scalp.

He set one big hand on her shoulder, tight, and held her still. He added another sluice of water.

Her heart thudded as water rained over her face. Not since she'd been a child had anyone washed her hair.

And then his fingers were in the strands, rubbing more suds, massaging, his big fingertips moving around her ears, her nape, and over her crown.

He was so gentle and unhurried that the tension in her shoulders seeped away. She blew out a breath and hugged her knees.

"Your hair is the color of the sun," he said in as soft a voice as she'd heard him use.

He said nothing more but continued to carefully wash her hair from behind.

Ingrid listened to the crackle of the fire and enjoyed the warm water soaking her skin. Still he kept on, leaving no section of her scalp without attention. When he'd done that, he took the long strands between his palms and rubbed.

Finally, he appeared satisfied, and as briskly as he'd tipped the first jug over her head, repeated the action.

She held still.

He did it again, and again, rinsing the suds from her locks.

"You are clean now," he said. "This is much better."

"Aye, thank you."

"Do not thank me. It is my job to care for you. I am the Viking of this house and you the maiden."

"So you keep saying." She wiped the water from her eyes. "But before you arrived, I cared for myself perfectly well."

"That is up for judgement." He stood. "Get out now."

She looked around. "Hand me that blanket and then face away."

His eyebrows pulled low, and his jaw tensed. A small muscle flexing beneath the skin.

"Gunnar." She gestured to the blanket.

He hesitated for a moment then passed it to her.

After taking it, she waited for him to avert his eyes.

He clicked his tongue on the roof of his mouth, something she'd noticed he did when frustrated, and turned so his broad, bare back was facing her.

Quickly she stood, water running from her body, and stepped out of the tub to stand beside the fire. She wrapped the blanket around her shoulders, hugging it close.

He faced her, his eyes narrowed and his lips damp as though he'd just swiped his tongue over them.

"I am going to my bed," she said. She'd made a plan earlier to get on it before him. Another night sleeping on the bench didn't appeal.

"Bed," he said, his voice gruff. "Aye." He hooked his thumb into the twist of the blanket sitting low on his hips and tugged.

The material fell to the floor, pooling around his feet.

She snatched in a breath.

His cock was hard and erect, the wide, smooth head glossy. His balls hung heavy, his thigh muscles taut, and his abdomen a wall of muscle.

Her throat constricted, and she swallowed, making a small gulping sound.

"It is time," he said, wrapping his fist around his thick shaft. "For the needs I talked of earlier to be satisfied."

Chapter Five

"Needs," Ingrid repeated in a tense whisper.

"Aye, needs." He took three strides so he was standing right before her. "I am a Viking, you are a maiden. Over this long winter I will bed you many times." His gaze drifted over her face as if seeing it for the first time. "That thought pleases me now we have bathed, so we will start."

"But...I..." Her heart was thudding. Her cunny quivered. Didn't he understand how big he was? How her cunny would never take his cock? "You are..."

"Ah!" He held up his finger and touched it to her lips. "I understand your concern."

Her lips prickled as though super-sensitive to contact with him.

"I am not your husband." He nodded. "I understand that, so for this first time you may wear this."

He reached to the table and plucked up a soft black length of material she used to wrap around her neck when working outside in the cold. He held it taut in front of her face.

What is he doing?

Stepping behind her, his soap-tinged body heat wafting around her, he placed the scarf over her eyes.

Blackness.

"Now you cannot see my face," he said beside her ear as he secured it in a knot over her damp hair. "So you can think of your husband's face if that is your desire. You can remember him doing to you what I am about to."

Oh, for the love of all the gods.

"I'm sure," he said in a gravelly murmur, "you will soon remember how much you enjoyed laying with a man, your memories will return. This is what you were made for, wench, to give and receive pleasure of the flesh."

He took hold of the blanket, tugging it from her grasp, and slowly lifted it from her body. The soft sound of the material bunching on the table to her right coincided with cooler air embracing her nakedness.

His breath was warm on her shoulder, his solid chest brushing her upper back

"Ingrid," he said, "do not be so stiff." He rested his hands on the slight flare of her hips. "I have no desire to hurt you, but you must help me by relaxing."

A tremble started in her belly and shivered upward to her chest, her neck, and then her teeth.

His thick, hot arms wrapped around her. Any chance of escape had gone. She was his. He'd made that plain as day. She was his to bed whenever he wanted over this long winter.

I should scream, fight, protest.

But Ingrid didn't. Within her black world there was something growing. A need and desire of her own. The craving to be satisfied by something other than her own fingers was getting bigger with each heartbeat.

"Over here." He maneuvered her to the bed, his hard cock brushing her bare buttocks. "Lie down."

She used her hands to feel her way onto the fur-thrown mattress, then lay flat, staring at the nothingness of the scarf over her eyes. Her nipples were tight, her skin still flushed from bathing.

"Ah, you are thin, but there is beauty there," he said. "I can see that now."

Beauty.

The bed dipped as he moved next to her. His body coming into alignment with hers. The feel of hot male skin after so long sleeping alone was new and strangely exciting.

His fingertip brushed her lips.

She let out a small gasp, not expecting him to touch her face.

But he continued. He traced the outline of her lips—she held her breath—then down her chin and around her jawline.

He was so close he seemed to surround her, fill her just with his presence.

"Breathe," he murmured hotly beside her ear. "And feel."

His caress down her neck to her throat was so light it was hard for her to imagine it was the same rough brute who'd tipped her over his knee for a spanking. Now his touch was a light as a kitten's whisker.

Which somehow made it all the more intense.

Her breaths were shallow now. He made his way to her right nipple, a trail of heat following in its wake.

When he circled it, she gripped the blanket beneath her. Her nipple tightened, hardened, and her entire breast, though small, became heavy.

"So sweet," he said, tugging it slightly. "So responsive." He stilled. "Ah, but I will not speak, then you can think of your husband without the reminder of my voice."

Frode had never been farther from Ingrid's mind. He'd never laid her down after bathing and stroked her this way. The few times he'd bedded her it had been functional, little else.

Gunnar moved to her opposite breast and tweaked that nipple the same way he had the other.

Ingrid bit on her bottom lip and held in a moan. It rumbled in her throat. It was as if a length of string went from her nipple to her cunny. The tug was insistent and strong, creating dampness between her thighs.

Which is where Gunnar's inquisitive fingers were heading now. Over her belly and to her mound of pale hair.

His lips grazed her shoulder, his jawline porcelain-smooth.

He delved deeper between her thighs.

Ingrid curled her toes and pressed her legs together.

"Let me in," he said, his journey more insistent, so insistent she had no choice but to widen her legs.

"Ah, hot cunny," he said, seeming to forget about not speaking. "This is what my cock needs."

But he didn't ease his cock into her wetness. Instead, he pressed one thick finger into her, his way eased by her slickness.

Ingrid gasped and reached for his forearm, gripped it.

He penetrated higher, the heel of his hand lodging against her swollen bud.

"Oh!" She clenched around him, her inner thighs trembling and her knees falling wider.

This seemed to encourage him, and he added another finger and rocked his hand, rubbing her, filling her.

She arched her back, glad of the blackness now. It meant all she had to do was feel. And what Gunnar was doing to her cunny was amazing, better than she could do it herself. His fingers were big and a little cool, the heel of his hand wide and solid.

Still she gripped his forearm, not wanting him to stop now. "Oh."

His breaths had quickened. His erect cock was trapped between them.

"Don't stop," she gasped. The familiar pressure was growing low in her belly. Except it wasn't familiar. She had no control over it. Gunnar had ownership of her pleasure, he was the one creating the rising tension that would soon spill over.

Another gush of moisture leaked around his fingers.

He moaned and latched his hot mouth over her right nipple, his teeth grazing it.

Ingrid cried out, it was sensation overload. He was consuming her, all she could think of. Even her love for the gods had faded. She barely knew which land she lived on.

Gunnar kept up the friction, his fingers going deep into her on each rock.

Ingrid basked in the moment before release. It was growing so big, so powerful. She held her breath, her body held hostage by him. He was playing her, as though he a fine craftsman and she his material.

"I'm...oh...don't stop...please."

And then a wondrous rush of pleasure burst from her cunny and spread over her body. She curled forward, her frame as taut as a bow about to fire an arrow.

He stayed with her, working her cunny, extending the moment, drawing out her bliss.

She called out again, incoherent words that even she didn't understand. Bright lights flashed behind her closed lids. She was lost to her own sublime world of satisfaction.

He released her breast, leaving her nipple hard and wet.

Dragging in a breath, she allowed her head to flop back to the furs.

"Now it is time for my pleasure," he said, withdrawing his fingers from her cunny.

She whimpered at the loss.

But then he was over her, his big bulk heavy and pressing onto her body, forcing her to keep her legs wide.

His cock was at her entrance. Impossibly big and solid, he pushed in.

Her breath hitched, and she clasped his shoulders, his muscles like rocks beneath her fingertips.

He pushed again, his cock determined and thick as it parted her delicate wet flesh.

She was still panting, still trembling from her orgasm. He curled his hips and entered her deeper.

"Oh...oh...Gunnar," she cried.

"Gunnar," he grunted. "You said my name."

"Aye. Gunnar, Gunnar...oh...oh..."

Suddenly her world brightened. He'd dragged the scarf from her eyes.

She stared into his face hovering over hers. His dark eyes were intense; storms raged within them.

"You are not thinking of your husband?" he growled out.

"No. Only you, you're...oh." How could she think of anything other than Gunnar at this moment? He was easing his huge cock into her quivering cunny with steely determination. Parting her flesh, claiming her, filling her.

He placed his palm over her forehead, moving the damp strands of hair from her brow. The other he set on the fur beside her left ear, elbow locked. His mouth was a tight line, as though he'd harnessed his self-control and was forcing himself to go slow.

She reached for his face, cupped his jawline, and stared into his eyes, grateful that he wasn't hurting her, that he was taking his time, allowing her body to accept his.

And it was, she was, he was almost at full depth. She'd taken him, her moisture easing his way as he'd sank deep.

Then, with a grunt, he curled his hips and went the rest of the way.

She gasped at a stitch of pain, and her eyes widened.

"Ah, you are as snug as a virgin," he said gruffly. "Your cunny hugging my cock as if it had never felt one before."

Truly, Ingrid never had felt one like Gunnar's before. His hot hardness was so dense inside her, so invasive yet so right.

"You will find pleasure again," he said, his nostrils flaring. "With me."

"Aye...I...oh...I want..."

"I know what you want." He half withdrew then slid in again, his body rubbing up and over her bud.

"Oh!" She pulled up her knees, clasping them to his torso. "Aye. Like that."

He didn't reply, just repeated the action, then again and again. All the time staring down at her, watching her face for every expression.

"Gunnar," she said breathily.

His eyes flashed, the storms within them whirling and tossing. "With me…"

"Aye…oh…"

The pressure was reaching dizzying heights again. The way he was grinding against her and filling her with each rock of his hips had her orgasm blooming. A beautiful spring flower about to unfurl in all its glory.

He sped up, his weight dropping heavier onto her body. This spun her to a point of no return, her delicate spot storing an avalanche of ecstasy about to tumble.

For some reason she gripped his ears, tugging them she bowed her back and gave in to her release.

He roared, plunging deeper than before, and joined her in pleasure.

Her cunny spasmed around his cock, tight fists of satisfaction as she struggled to catch her breath.

Over and over, he filled her with heat, and she welcomed every slick ride of his cock. Her pleasure extended in a way it never had before. Her body barely felt like her own.

"Aye…thanks be to the gods." He rose, locking both arms, and looked down at where they'd joined.

Ingrid followed his line of sight.

Their flesh was slick with sweat, his hair-coated skin dark and battle-marked, hers pale and fragile in comparison, her breasts small peaks topped with tight nipples.

"I had forgotten on my travels," he said gruffly, "how pleasing it is to lay with a woman."

She didn't reply. How could she? This was, after all, the first time she'd lain with a man and been given pleasure. Extreme pleasure.

She didn't regret Gunnar taking her body, not one bit. But she did regret reaching the age she was without experiencing a skilled Viking man in her bed, one who truly wanted to be inside her.

He shuddered and curled his hips again, as if checking he'd entered her as deep as he could. His cock was still hard.

She fluttered her eyes closed, a thick sense of satisfaction taking her in its hold.

"We have all winter," he said, "Gods willing, and I will claim you that way many times, and Ingrid, I promise you will never be left wanting. Not by me."

"I believe you," she said.

A slight grin tugged his mouth, and for a moment she saw a flash of male pride, or was it smugness, in his eyes.

And then he withdrew and flopped at her side with one arm flung over his head. He let out a deep exhale.

Ingrid did the same, a final shudder rippling over her belly as she clamped her legs together. She stared up at the mended roof, the familiar rattle of the wind shaking the door in its frame.

After a few minutes, her eyes grew heavy then closed. Blackness surrounded her, and she allowed herself to drift off to sleep, her thoughts scattering, a warm fur settled over her, taking away the chill that had been growing on her flesh.

She sighed, feeling safe and content for the first time in a long time.

Chapter Six

"While there is daylight, woman, I will go and set traps." Gunnar flicked up the thickly furred hood on his heavy cloak. "And when I return, we will eat, and I will bed you, so see to the animals and prepare our eve."

"I'm already preparing," Ingrid said, raising her eyebrows at him and her mouth twitching into a smile as she kneaded dough. She wasn't going to complain if he wanted to bed her again, he had every night since that first encounter, a total of three times now, and she was happy for more.

He scooped up two rusting steel traps that he'd brought with him. "Do not forget the animals."

"I will not forget them." How could she? They were too important. Their eggs and milk relied upon. And now the barn roof had also been mended, they were happier and warmer.

He grunted and stomped past her. For a moment she wondered if he would pause and kiss her. He did not.

She was yet to feel his lips on hers. Oh, she knew what his cock felt like inside her, his mouth on her nipples, but nothing more. Not the press of his tongue on hers or his taste.

"And," he stopped at the door, his big hand against it, "when you go to the barn, take that dagger." He gestured to a sharp blade with a slim bone handle he'd set on the barrel of mead.

"Why?" She frowned. As if she didn't have enough to carry and remember.

"I heard a wolf's call in the night, it wasn't far away, and now the snow is here they will be getting ever more hungry."

"They have never come to the barn."

"There is a first time." His eye's narrowed. "You will do as I have instructed so you always have a weapon." He paused. "Do you hear me?"

"Aye, I hear you. Though a dagger against a hungry wolf is like shaking a feather at a serpent."

"It is better than naught, and I do not want you to be caught without something to slice its throat should the need arise." He made a cutting motion at his neck. "Go for it here."

"I will not see a wolf, I assure you. They live yonder, over to the east of the forest."

"Ingrid!" His roar blasted around the longhouse.

Ingrid jumped within her skin and stopped kneading. She swallowed.

"You!" He pointed at her. "Will do as you are told or in the name of all the gods you will pay the price. Take the dagger when you leave these walls."

He spun around. The door slammed. A swirl of snow danced in on the stiff wind and settled where his big boots had just been.

Dagger, I have to take the dagger.

She sighed, her breath a little shaky, and continued to knead.

Not having a grumbling stomach was still a novelty, and already her energy had increased from eating more nourishment. Gunnar's arrival had satisfied her in many ways.

Ingrid hummed, a horn tune she'd heard for the first time on her wedding day, many years ago. She wondered if Tove had also had music played at her wedding.

She worked the bread and her heartstrings tugged. She missed her daughter dreadfully and hoped her new life was pleasing. That her new husband, the king, was treating her well both in and out of the bedchamber. Would she fall with child quickly? Would she only ever have one like she, Ingrid?

All of these questions spun in her mind. Ingrid set the bread aside then headed out to the barn to feed the animals.

For once the snow had eased, and though the sky hung heavy with clouds there was a break on the horizon with the thin-arced sliver of the sun peeking through it. It was as high as it would rise today before returning to hours of slumber. The sun was missed greatly and its return to the skies a reason to celebrate.

"Hey, girls," Ingrid said, entering the barn.

A slew of bleats and clucks rang out.

Gunnar's horse, Bo, was absent, his big hoof marks setting a trail east as Gunnar had ridden out with the traps.

As she fed the chickens and then stuffed the troughs with fresh hay brought from Halsgrof, she wondered about the west. Gunnar had spoken of winters with the sun awake each day and ground that was rich with life, rivers and lochs that didn't freeze.

Ingrid could barely imagine this. All her life she'd spent the winter season in virtual hibernation, hunkering down, fighting the cold, battling to survive on rations.

"Maybe one day," she said to her goats. "Maybe one day Gunnar will take me there."

Bah.

She smiled and knocked ice from the water pail then filled Bo's hay trough in preparation for his return.

With a bit of luck, Gunnar's traps would be successful and they'd eat well for a few days, dry some meat, too, and boost their supply shelves.

Her breath huffed into the air as she scooped soiled straw and pushed it to the side of the barn with her pitchfork. The handle was smooth and worn from years of use. It had been a present from her father on her wedding day, he'd made it with his own hands, despite his knuckles being stiff.

It had been years since she'd seen him. Was he even alive?

For the first time in many moons, she had a little spark of hope. 'Haps Gunnar would fix Frode's boat, and in the spring she could row up the fjord and see him, her mother, too. Oh, what news she had about their granddaughter being queen. Aye, they should hear that, they'd swell with pride, perhaps even journey to visit the king and queen, if they were well enough.

She carried on with her work, another little tune catching on her breaths, a happy, hopeful sound that warmed her from the inside out. Her fortunes had changed when she'd sent Tove to line up before King Njal, a decision that had been hard to make, but ultimately, the right one for her family.

She checked again for eggs. There were none, Gunnar had gathered two earlier. Two of the goats were in need of milking, so she did that, though the new ram, sent by Tove, was a nuisance, butting her, and eventually she had to tie him to the cartwheel. "Make yourself useful." She nodded at the two goats who had yet to produce. "And then you might not end up in a broth."

He bleated at her, his little pink tongue poking out and indignation flashing in his eyes.

She chuckled and carried on working in the light of an oil lamp she kept permanently on. When she'd finished, she gathered her basket, placed the milk jug inside, and left the barn.

The slice of sun had long gone, and darkness spread over the white-coated land in a thick woolen cloak. After bolting the barn door, she gathered her skirt and headed for the longhouse.

Smoke was still trickling from the chimney. She'd stacked the fire well and would again as soon as she was back. Being warm and with a good stash of candles were other luxuries she was enjoying.

Suddenly, a shadow slinked from the edge of the far end of the barn. It grew larger, bigger, showing its shape stretched on the snowy earth.

Pointed face, mean hunched shoulders, long ragged back, tail, four strong legs.

Wolf.

Ingrid's heart stuttered, and she stilled with her pulse thudding in her ears and her mouth drying.

The creature came into view, standing over the boot prints—hers and Gunnar's—leading to the barn. The cunning animal had blocked her way to the longhouse.

Their eyes locked.

The wolf peeled back its lips, snarling, exposing wet pink gums, huge teeth, and a string of drool. Its eyes flashed in the snowy winter light.

"Get out of here!" she snapped, hoping she sounded braver than she felt.

It took a step closer, head lowered, growling now. Its hackles raised like needles along its back.

Ingrid glanced over her shoulder. Could she make a dash back to the barn, unlock it, and get inside before the creature pounced?

She didn't know.

But she'd have to try.

Her legs were shaking, her belly tense. Fear rattled her bones, and panic scalded her blood.

She'd throw the basket as a distraction and then run as fast as she could through the deep snow. She didn't fancy her chances—three bounds and it would be on her.

And then another shadow loomed from the side of the barn. Huge and wide and approaching fast.

A roar—deep and primitive and blood-curdling.

The wolf spun around with its hackles still upended.

"AHHHHH! GET OUT OF HERE!" Gunnar's voice boomed so loud it would have been enough to start an avalanche had he been at the pass.

He roared again, the way a bear would, his mouth wide and eyes wild.

The wolf hunched a little lower, front legs dipping. It stopped snarling, and its tail drooped. Its teeth were still bared.

Gunnar stormed toward it without a grain of fear in his movements. Not a flicker of hesitation in his eyes.

Ingrid backed up, gripping the basket until her knuckles hurt. Her stomach was a tight knot of terror and her breaths shallow. What was he doing? The wolf would attack, surely. Likely there were more of them, too. It would be a bloodbath. Gunnar's blood, then hers.

"Go on. Go!" Gunnar shouted, unsheathing a wickedly sharp dagger and holding it high in his left hand. "Get out of here! Now!"

Snow-light glanced off the blade.

The wolf took a step back, not fast, as though he was undecided what to do about the massive menacing creature yelling and approaching.

This indecisiveness seemed to annoy Gunnar all the more, and he sped up, rounding his shoulders, his bulky cloak doubling his size as it flapped.

The wolf turned, a gush of white bursting up from its huge paws, and then sped off into the night, the crunch of its feet on snow fading fast.

Gunnar made as if to chase, seven, eight, nine rapid strides, all accompanied by a furious bellow. He raised his arms in the air, tall as a pier tower, and shook his fists, the dagger pointed at the gods.

Ingrid blew out a breath. Her hands were trembling, so were her knees. The wolf had gone. Certain death no longer imminent. Gunnar had arrived and saved her.

"Gunnar," she managed shakily.

He lowered his arms and turned. From beneath his hood, he glowered at her.

"Thanks be to Odin," she said, pressing her hand to her chest over her red cloak.

"Where is yours?" He shook the dagger her way. "Tell me. Now."

"My what?"

Ingrid knew full well what he was talking about. She gulped, knowing she'd disobeyed but only just realizing she had.

"Don't act dim-witted, you know what I am saying." He stepped up to her, slipping his dagger into the sheath at his waist. "Where is your weapon? The one I instructed you to have on your person when coming to tend the animals."

"My weapon?" She held the basket in front of herself, shield-like.

"Aye, wench, your weapon." He was right in front of her, staring at her, dark flashes of anger searing over his irises. His voice was low and dangerous, resembling the rumble of rocks before they slid down a mountainside.

"I...I...do not—"

"Have it," he finished for her. "I can see that." He swiped at her cloak, parting it so he could see her empty belt.

She lost her grip on the basket. It tumbled to the ground, the milk spilling.

"Did I not make myself clear?" He loomed over her.

Now she knew why the wolf had run, why its courage had deserted it. Gunnar's roar was loud, his anger tangible, and now its focus was all on her.

"I am sorry," she said. Had she ever felt so small?

"Sorry!" he shouted. "Sorry, what good would that do when your head had been ripped from your neck, woman? No good at all." He gritted his teeth, his lips peeling back in a snarl. "You have disobeyed me, to the extent it could have cost you your life."

"I was going to run, to the barn and—"

"And you never would have made it. That wolf was skinny and hungry, you would have been a good meal, then his pack would have made short work of the livestock."

He stooped, ducked, and shoved his shoulder against her belly.

The next thing Ingrid knew, she was hoisted upward and plonked over his shoulder. Her legs were high, her head hanging down. "Gunnar! Argh!"

His hand landed hard over her bottom, pinning her in place. "Keep still, woman." He turned, whistled. "Bo! Get!"

She huffed out air as he took a few large heavy paces to the barn and pulled the door open. "Please, put me down."

"Bo! Get here, wolf has gone."

There was a rush of wind and the swoosh of hooves on snow. Bo had made a swift entry into the barn.

Blood rushed to Ingrid's head. She grabbled to hang on to Gunnar's cloak, trying to steady herself.

"This eve could have turned in a very different direction." Gunnar shut the door, locking them into the barn with the animals. "As it is, you're still going to get a different eve to what you'd thought."

"But please, I..." Suddenly she was being lowered to the dusty floor, but no sooner had her feet hit it, she was once again being dragged down, over his knee this time, bottom in the air, head low. "Oh!"

"You will feel my hand for this, wench, and you *will* have learned your lesson by the time I am finished."

"Oh no, please, Gunnar, I won't forget the dagger again, I will always have it with me, I—"

"It is only a sore red rump that will ensure your obedience on this matter." He shoved at her cloak, pushing it up and over her shoulders. "And I can assure you it will be very sore, you'll nay be sitting for a week once I'm done with you, wench."

Chapter Seven

Indignation and humiliation swarmed within Ingrid. She clenched her jaw and kicked her heels up.

"Stop that, wench." He batted her legs down, her right boot slipping off and to the floor with a *whump*.

The chickens clucked wildly at the skirmish in their barn, and the ram bleated, long and high-pitched.

"You cannot do this, you...oh!"

He'd pulled her undergarment up, exposing her bare bottom. Cold air washed over her flesh.

"You big brute, you have no right to..." She wriggled with more energy but to no avail. "You can't..."

"I will do as I wish with you. I am master of this longhouse, master of this farmstead, and master of you." He scooped her close, trapping her against his solid body. "Now take your punishment with dignity."

"No, I...argh!" She jolted forward.

He'd swiped his palm over her buttocks, both of them, hard. The sting was instantly burning and the pain deep into her muscle.

She clenched her cheeks and arched her back.

He struck again, the burning pain more extreme because she'd tensed.

"No!" she cried, fisting his pants. "No more." How could she stand this? He was putting solid Viking muscle into the strikes. His hand so wide he was catching her slender bottom almost entirely with each spank.

"Aye, more," he growled. He pushed her shoulders so she was upended once again. "Until I believe you to have learned your lesson."

He spanked her again, and again. The slaps coming swiftly one after another, no break between them.

The sound was shocking as it sliced through the barn. Each spank dragging a squeal from her that added to the noise.

Spank. Spank. Spank.

Heat rushed up her spine and over her scalp. It spread between her legs, to her cunny, dampening her there, then down her inner thighs. With the burn was a swarm of bees, stinging and stinging, layering up the pain.

"Gunnar!" she cried, tears streaming over her face. "Please. Stop."

To her surprise he did, and he set his work-roughened hand over her buttocks, applying a firm pressure to her sore skin.

"You really do make a festival out of a spanking," he said a little breathlessly. "You are not making this easy on yourself."

"Enough now. Leave me be."

He kind of chuckled, a gruff, low noise in his throat. "And you think it is wise to tell me what to do while you are over my knee with your little bottom right beneath my nose and at my mercy?"

She grunted in frustration and once again tried to free herself. It was no good. In fact, he held her all the tighter.

He smoothed his hand over her cheeks, first the right, then the left, as though examining the results of his punishment on her poor behind.

Her flesh was on fire and super-sensitive.

And then he dipped lower, through the cleft of her buttocks, over her rear hole and to her cunny.

"Oh!" She stilled. She was so wet there, she didn't know why, and now he was going to know that fact. Embarrassment sent a new wave of heat through her blood, and she clamped her legs together.

But it was no good, his determined fingers buried into her cunny, slipping in easily because of her moisture.

"Oh, Ingrid, you are a disgrace," he said. "And your body is telling me everything."

"It tells you naught. Leave me be." She held her breath as he tunneled deeper, wiggling his fingers into her cunny and stroking there.

The dense filling sent a longing for more through her abdomen, and her bud tingled. She arched her back, tipping her butt to seat her cunny more thoroughly onto him. A low moan escaped her throat.

"You are not supposed to be enjoying this." He withdrew, and in an instant the spanking had resumed. Even harder and faster than before.

She cried out with each slap of his hand over her tender skin.

Sweat prickled on her brow, and her cunny tightened so much a slick of fluid slid to her inner thighs. Her nipples peaked. The pain ran amok around her body.

I hate him, in the name of all the gods, I hate this man.

The tears resumed, hot and angry drips over her temples and then the floor. She couldn't take any more. She was so slight, he so big, and he seemed to have forgotten that.

Finally, he slowed, but there was still power behind the spanks, and then he stopped.

She was breathing hard, so was he.

Her behind was on fire, the air bitterly cold against the scorched skin.

"You will not forget your weapon again, wench."

"No. No, never. I will always carry it." She sniffed and dashed at her damp nose. "I promise, in the name of Odin and Freya, I promise that."

"And if you break that promise? If you put yourself at risk, what will happen?"

She hesitated.

"Tell me!"

"I will be over your knee again, for a spanking."

"A spanking harder than this one, and for longer, you hear, and I will plug your rear hole with a candle so every time my hand lands you will grip it until it near snaps."

"Gunnar!" His words shocked her, but instantly she knew he would carry out his threat. "No, please...let me be."

"And what will you do when I let you be?"

"I just...I just want to...oh!"

Suddenly, she was being hoisted up and over his knees. She slid to the floor, no strength in her legs, landing beside a pile of clean animal bedding. The straw scratched her poor buttocks, and she whimpered, closing her eyes.

"My woman." He caught her chin. "You nearly died because of your disobedience." He paused. "Look at me."

She peeled her eyes open and was surprised at how close his face was to hers. His cheeks were red, his pupils wide.

"If I had not returned when I did, you would not be breathing at my side now."

"I know that." She sniffed. "I feel so foolish, but there has never been wolf at the barn before and—"

"Enough, it does not matter what you think, what has happened here before my arrival." He gripped her upper arms and leaned low. "Everything has changed now that I am with you. Everything, do you understand that?"

"Aye, aye, I understand." Her voice was shaky, her heart racing.

He kind of grunted and released her arms. He stood.

She slid to her side, her strength leaving her. Her elbow buried into the straw, and she was grateful for it covering the hard floor.

He turned away from her and removed his cloak, dropping it beside the cartwheel.

Bo was watching him, chewing lazily on his hay.

Ingrid squeezed her legs together. Her body was on fire, her cunny fluttering, and her sensitive spot swollen.

He balled his fists and dragged in a deep breath, his wide shoulders lifting, his back expanding.

She watched him warily. What was he going to do next? Unlike Frode, Gunnar was completely unpredictable. She couldn't guess if he was going to storm from the barn, spank her again, or start milking the goats.

"You." He turned and set his hands on his hips. "Are likely the most frustrating, tempting, disobedient, beautiful woman I have ever met."

"Beautiful?" It was the only word she'd heard. "Me?"

"Aye." He frowned. "And your cunny..."

"W...what about it?" Warm slickness remained, and she was very aware of it. "What about my cunny?"

"It reacts to a spanking the way it does to my cock."

"But..." Shame swarmed around her. "I hated the spanking." She pushed at her tunic, covering her legs.

His mouth flattened, and he narrowed his eyes. "You cannot deny or hide what is a truth, your cunny is wet with desire."

She swallowed, her throat tight. Her inner thighs pulsed, and a needy weight filled her pelvis. "No, I cannot deny it."

In two fast paces he was in front of her. Wildness flared in his eyes, and a vein in his temple throbbed. "On order of the king and queen, you are my responsibility, and I will not have you wanting." He dropped to his knees at her feet. "It is my duty to protect, punish, *and* pleasure you."

"Pleasure me?"

"Aye." He snatched the base of her tunic and shoved it upward, once again exposing her thighs and then the triangle of hair at the juncture of her legs. A muscle flexed in his cheek. "Pleasure."

He set his big palms on her thighs and spread them wide.

Cool air gushed over her exposed cunny. "Oh! Gunnar...what..."

He was staring at her soft folds with hunger and determination etched onto his handsome features.

She gasped and clutched handfuls of straw. What was he going to do?

"You are so wet I can see you dripping."

Her cheeks flushed. No man had ever stared at her cunny this way, and when she knew she was swollen and glistening with arousal, it made it all the more toe-curling.

But then Ingrid had no more time to be ashamed because Gunnar leaned forward and nuzzled his face between her legs.

"Oh!" She stared at his wide shoulders and the plait running over his head. "Oh...in the name of Freya...I..."

He laved over her delicate flesh, tasting her, exploring with the tip of his tongue. He then set his tongue over her sweet bud and rotated it with a firm pressure.

She snatched in a breath. She stopped seeing, her mind focused only on the sensation he was creating within her. It was incredible. Deep and intimate. Wild and wanton.

He dropped lower as if he couldn't get close enough and used his fingers to toy with her entrance.

Ingrid's strength left her, and she flopped onto her back, her eyes closing as she struggled to breathe. She'd forgotten all about her smarting bottom.

He was pushing her toward a rapid climax. One she knew would take her to dizzying heights.

Her cunny was filled with two of his fingers, and she gripped him, holding on. She rushed toward release.

He didn't let up, working her with his mouth, driving her onward.

Suddenly, the pressure became too much. She held her breath, bowed her back, and savored the sweet moment before she gave in to it.

"Ah!" she cried out. Bliss exploded from her cunny and blasted through her body. It ravaged her nerves, solidified her muscles, and flashed brilliant bright lights over her eyelids. She clamped her legs to his shoulders and pressed down onto him, wanting more, wanting it all, everything he had to give.

He stayed with her, pounding his fingers into her cunny and giving her what she needed as she spasmed and pulsed and cried out.

"Gunnar...oh, Odin, Thor, and Freya..." she gasped. "That is..."

He lifted, his mouth shiny and his fingers still inside her.

"You...what you just did," she managed. "I have never...no one has ever..."

His mouth twisted into a wicked half-smile. "Then it is about time someone did. I thank the gods it was me." He stroked her insides, right where the sensation was at its densest.

She groaned, and her eyes fluttered closed again; it was so good. He was so good.

He kind of chuckled. "I swear you are the sweetest wench to both punish and pleasure, Ingrid."

She didn't reply, she was in awe of his skill, of his ability to play her body like a master toolmaker. Silently, she thanked the All Father for sending him to her that winter's night. She thanked all the gods for making Tove queen and for King Njal's generosity.

The thought of not having Gunnar with her now, even if his spankings did pain her, wasn't one she could entertain.

"Much as I could play with your honeyed cunny all night, wench," Gunnar said, sliding his fingers from her and sitting back on his heels, "I am hungry for food, for bread and fish."

She drew her legs together, feeling puffy with pleasure. The scent of her arousal drifted upward. "Aye. I have prepared it for you." She was still breathless.

"Good." He stood and held out his hand for her.

She took it, allowing him to tug her to standing. Her clothing fell into place.

He caught her face in his palms. "You will not forget that spanking."

"No."

"And you will not forget to carry a weapon."

"No, Gunnar. I will not."

"Because if you do." He paused and gritted his teeth. "I will—"

"I know what you'll do, you told me." How could she forget?

He nodded once.

She stared at his mouth. His lips were soft and wide, and he'd allowed a small patch of hair beneath the bottom one to sprout over the last week. Everything in her body, her mind, told her to reach up and kiss him, press her mouth to his. To join their souls as man and woman.

But something stopped her. It wasn't her place to kiss him. Gunnar was master, and it was for him to decide if and when they should kiss.

Oh, but I want him to.

He released her face and turned to reach for his cloak. "Come, we will go to the longhouse and sit by the fire as we eat."

Chapter Eight

Several days passed. Gunnar got lucky with his traps and brought two gutted white hares for her to cook. He'd declared a plan to track a deer—he'd come across hoof prints.

Ingrid's bottom remained tender. Her punishment for forgetting the dagger had been harsh, and she was reminded of it every time she sat. But Gunnar's methods had worked, she hadn't forgotten the dagger once since he'd tipped her over his knee. The dagger was attached to the belt on her tunic whenever she left the longhouse.

The new ram had been busy with the young ewes, and Ingrid had every hope there'd be new life in the spring. She thought of this, sitting stitching a hole in a pair of socks, and wondered at her own belly. Would she swell with child? Gunnar's seed filled her frequently, much more than Frode's ever had.

Ingrid sent a silent request to Freya, asking for a babe. She was still fertile. As each full moon came around, she bled. 'Haps she would become a mother again, the mother of Gunnar's warrior son.

She smiled. The thought pleased her very much.

"What are you thinking of?" Gunnar asked, sipping mead from a horn and leaning back on his chair.

"Naught."

"It is something. Tell me."

"I was thinking of...Tove, wondering if she was with child."

"I am sure she will be. King Njal is a virile Viking, she will give him many sons." He paused. "You wish to be with her, when she gives birth?"

"Aye, it is a mother's place."

"In which case, in the spring, I will take you to the town. You can hear news with your own ears."

She set down her stitching. "I would like that, Gunnar, but who would care for the animals if I am not here?"

"When we arrive at Halsgrof, I will pay a farmer's boy a silver coin to come and care for them, until we return. He can plant crops, too. Tend the land."

"We?"

"Aye." He took a drink then closed his eyes, leaning his head back against the tall-backed chair. "I am thinking this will be a nice place during the summer season. When the sun does not sleep."

"You are right." She picked up her stitching again and squinted at it through the candlelight. "When the wind blows from the south, the waves lap in small whispers against the pebbles. The grass sways as if dancing, and the birds sing day and night, rejoicing in their wings, the seeds, and the sun on their feathers. Fish are plentiful when the boat is taken yonder, around the big rock shaped like a shield, and the earth gives greens in every shade." She sighed, thinking of the summer and how life became easier with the break from cold winds and ice. When the sun gave heat to her bones and painted her skin like a tanned hide.

"You sell it very well," he said. "'Haps I'll have a break from journeying overseas, set my roots here for a while."

Ingrid said nothing. Was Gunnar serious or was he speaking this way because it was the depths of winter, and like many of the animals in the forest he was tired, hibernating almost? Doing what he needed to stay warm and eat and little else.

Except bedding me. He does a lot of that.

Smiling, she reached for the poker and stoked the fire. When her sore bottom had healed, she'd be quite content. So far, she was wintering much better than she'd ever dared hope. Food and fuel and Viking company—handsome Viking company—who made her heart speed up each time he returned from his traps, each time he stepped into the longhouse, every time he entered her body.

* * * *

"Ingrid, come here!"

Ingrid paused milking her largest female goat. "I am busy."

"Stop what you are doing and come to my side, wench."

She sighed and put the pail down. She'd become used to obeying. In fact, it was the easiest thing to do. "I'll be right back," she said to the goat and wiped her hands on a rag.

She went out of the barn and into the cold darkness.

Gunnar stood there, hands on hips, staring into the distance.

She followed his line of sight.

Ribbons of pale-green, silver, and blue fluttered over the mountain crests, great waves of shifting, swaying light that billowed and snaked.

"The Valkyries' armor is reflecting so much tonight," Ingrid said, marveling at the sight.

"Aye, they must be leading many warriors over the Bifrost Bridge to the Great Hall."

"There has been a battle then," she said. "I wonder where."

"South, far south," he said, folding his arms. "Two Viking clans in dispute."

"How do you know?"

"It is the only explanation for this many slain warriors going to Valhalla."

"They will feast well with the gods tonight," Ingrid said. "We will raise a horn of mead to them and wish them well for having good deaths in battle."

"Aye, we will do that."

He turned to her, and she looked up at his face. The whispering lights seemed to reflect off the snow onto his skin, shadowing his nose and narrowed eyes.

Whenever she was near him, she had the urge to touch him, but she didn't. Instead, she stood stock-still.

"You are proving to be a fine woman," he said quietly.

"I am?" His words pleased her, any praise from him did.

"Aye, you understand the ways of a man and the ways of the gods, not all women do."

"I am trying."

"You are succeeding." He stepped a little closer, his chest only inches from her.

"It is good to hear you say that, Gunnar."

He nodded, a little stiffly, his eyes boring into hers. "Ingrid?"

"What are you asking?" she said quietly.

"I am...I'm not asking, I am going to do it." He cupped her face and lowered his head. His nose touched the tip of hers briefly, and then he was kissing her. Really kissing her, his lips moving on hers and his tongue pressing between her teeth.

She moaned softly and squeezed closer.

Her action set off a swift reaction in him, and he released her face and wrapped his arms around her waist, hauling her near. Tugging her to her tiptoes.

"Ingrid," he breathed against her mouth. "You want me to kiss you as a man kisses a woman's soul?"

"Aye, aye, I do." She slid her hands around his neck, holding on to him, using him as an anchor as her heart soared.

"Even though I am not your husband."

"My husband has been gone a long time, Gunnar, you are the man in my life now."

"Aye, that I am." Once again, his mouth hit down on hers, a passionate, determined kiss that stole her breath and had her body buzzing from her toes to the top of her head. Finally, she knew what his kiss held; after longing for it, she now had it.

He slipped his hands to her butt, and over her cloak he cupped her cheeks. And then he was lifting her.

Their kiss didn't break as she wrapped her legs around his waist and crossed her ankles in his lower back.

He moaned. His hard cock wedged up against her cunny through their clothing.

A gush of need ripped through her. This Viking who had knocked on her door in the midst of a storm had become her world, and she wanted him desperately.

"I need to be inside you," he said, backing up so her shoulders touched the barn wall. "And I am not wasting time going to the longhouse."

"Please," she said against his lips. "Take me, make me yours."

He kind of growled and shoved at his waistband, his belt falling to the snowy ground and his cock springing free. Next, he pushed her undergarments aside.

Cold air washed over her cunny, and she trembled with longing. Gunnar's swift, urgent movements had her panting with excitement. She'd never been so desired, so needed. It was intoxicating, as though she'd eaten the mushrooms that grew in the woodland yonder.

"Take my cock and my kisses," he said, angling the tip of his erection at her entrance.

"I want it all," she said, clinging to his shoulders and bracing for penetration. "All of you, everything."

"You've got me." He gritted his teeth and stared into her eyes. Then he curled his hips under and forced his cock deep.

She cried out, the sudden dense filling bringing a nip of pain as well as glorious satisfaction.

The sky lit behind him. He stilled whilst buried deep, allowing her to get used to the thick invasion. Waves of emerald, jade, and dandelion-yellow that flashed and flickered and galloped over the sky.

Canting her hips, she squeezed his cock with her cunny.

"Ah, my woman," he moaned, his eyes fluttering closed. He kissed her again and withdrew, only to pound back in, shoving her against the barn wall as he rode to full depth.

Ingrid hugged him, utterly lost to him, thoroughly owned by him.

His body ground up against her, and instantly, the yearning for more was there. She groaned into his mouth, her tongue slick against his.

Again he almost withdrew, then entered deep again. He set up a fast pace, seeming desperate to show her with his cock how much she meant to him. Prove their souls had intertwined.

Never in her life had Ingrid thought she would have sex outside, against the barn with a wild Viking warrior. She hadn't dared to dream, fantasize, but now it was happening, and it was real. "Oh. Oh. Oh." She huffed out breaths with each of his eager thrusts.

Soon the pressure had reached the delicious point where it needed to overspill, she couldn't contain it.

"With me," he gasped into her mouth. "I can feel you're there...your cunny is so tight and wet. Release with me...do it, give in to it...now."

She obeyed him and allowed bliss to explode through her. It was as raging as any bellow of thunder from the gods, as hot as fire, better than it had ever been.

He let out a roar and threw his head back to the sky. He pinned her to the barn with his body and his cock released his pleasure.

Ecstasy pulsed in her cunny, and her breaths were hard to catch. She could feel the engorged root of his cock throbbing.

He curled his hips under again. The barn wall creaked. "Aye, so...good. You feel so good."

"Gunnar." She clung to him as he eked out their pleasure. Ensuring every last drip of satisfaction had been claimed. "Oh aye, I love you."

He dropped his face to hers, and his eyes flashed. "You...you love me?" he asked.

"Aye." Her heart, though beating fast, stuttered, almost tripping over itself. Why had she said that? The words had just poured from her. "I do."

"Wench." He caught her chin in his hand. Hot air puffed from his mouth, billowing around them and mixing with hers. "Do not say that if you do not mean it."

"I *do* mean it." His hold on her chin was firm, and his cock was still buried deep. "I cannot imagine being here alone, without you."

"That is not love, that is because I provide for you."

"Gunnar." Her eyes tingled, threatening to mist and swell with tears. "That is not true, it is you I love, your Viking warrior heart."

He swallowed, a noisy gulp in the quiet night. "You speak the truth?"

"Aye, I promise."

His lips drew into a straight line.

For a moment she didn't think he'd speak, then, "Ingrid, you are mine, you are my woman in a way I have never had a woman before. You are..."

"I am what?"

He pressed closer, seeming to push his cock even deeper into her body. "You are the lights in the sky, the waves on this loch, the food I feast upon. You are everything to me, your smile, your obedience, your sweet kisses, and honeyed body...I love you, too."

"You do?"

"Aye, can you not tell?" He kissed her again, gentler this time, his lips telling her how much he adored her with each soft, stroking movement.

She lost where he stopped and she began, everything drifted away, the cold, the Valkyrie's flashing armor, the long, dark winter. For Ingrid, life had never been so warm, so whole, or so gratifying.

And it was all because of Gunnar of Barosvik, the Viking who loved her.

Chapter Nine

The days shortened until there was barely a few breaths of light each noon. The sun so shy it remained dipped beneath the mountains, sending only weak pink rays over the loch.

That nod to the passing of another day was as ghostly as it was bitterly cold. The loch had frozen and been layered up with snow so it was impossible to see where the land ended and water began.

Ingrid prepared food and tended the animals while Gunnar checked his traps, hunted, and fixed up the longhouse.

Life had become a rhythm of survival. Outside one storm raged after another, beating the sides of the barn, flapping any loose board on their home and stealing in beneath the door whenever it could.

But the nights weren't cold. With a constant fire flickering in the trough, and with an abundance of new blankets and furs, Ingrid stayed warm against Gunnar's body.

He made love to her frequently, sometimes twice a night, and each time he kissed her, soul-deep kisses that filled her with hope for the future.

Ingrid finished collecting eggs, five in total, and glanced at one of the young goats. She was standing in the corner, dozing, and while standing utterly still, it was clear her belly was swelling.

"Ah, this is good." Ingrid nodded at the ram. "Come spring we will have more goats and with that more milk."

Gunnar would be pleased, he drank lots of milk, always giving himself a white line on his top lip which he wiped away with the back of his hand.

"Woman!"

She spun around at the sound of Gunnar's voice. He'd been out in the darkness for hours checking traps.

"Woman! Where are you?"

She rushed to the barn door and opened it.

Bo loomed from the falling blanket of snow. Atop him sat Gunnar with his snow-peppered hood pulled up and his dark cloak fastened tight.

"I have slain a deer."

"You have?"

Gunnar drew closer and Ingrid spotted the gutted beast thrown behind him.

"We must prepare it and freeze it. We will eat well for Winterfest."

"That is good." She could already imagine the smell of the meat cooking. It was her very favorite meat and a long time since she'd indulged.

Once beside the barn, Gunnar allowed the carcass to fall to the ground. "I gutted it in the forest yonder, the wolves will have their fill. But I do not wish to attract them here, there is a big pack, the prints are evident."

She shuddered. "We do not want any more wolf visits." Her buttocks tingled just the memory of the last one. Her punishment for not carrying her dagger had been severe.

Now she reached for her dagger, and as Gunnar slid to his feet, she began to work.

Bo trotted into the barn, obviously keen for hay and warmth and glad the weight from his back had gone.

Together they worked, skinning the creature then butchering it into manageable pieces.

When they'd finished, Gunnar straightened. "You are skilled."

"Thank you. Frode used to leave me to this task whenever he had a successful hunt."

He raised his eyebrows. Several snowflakes had caught in them. "Your husband did not do it for you?"

"No."

A frown plowed over his brow. "Did he not care for you properly, Ingrid?"

She hesitated. "Aye, he cared for me."

"What are you not telling me?"

"Naught."

"Hmm." He straightened and wiped his hands on a rag. "You speak little of Frode, and I am beginning to think it is because he did little to ensure your wellbeing."

"That is not true." She bristled. It was not good to speak ill of the dead.

"There was disrepair here when I arrived, indeed his boat is still full of holes."

"He's been gone many summers."

"Aye, that is a point well made." He stepped close, his eyes set on her. "You believed him to be a good husband? Tell me that, woman. I need to know if he gave you what you need so when I meet him in Valhalla we can feast together as friends."

"Aye..." She couldn't hold his eye contact. "He did."

"Woman!"

She shivered. A cold gust of wind had circled her.

"Tell me." He lowered his face to hers. "Did he not provide enough food, enough fuel, enough animals or—"

"No, nothing like that. We lived well with Tove. We did."

"Winter, too?"

"Aye."

"He kept you warm in bed? Satisfied the way I do?"

Again she looked away for fear he'd see the sadness in her eyes—the memories of pleasuring herself because her husband had no interest in her body.

"Now I understand." He wrapped his arms around her, tugging her into the folds of his thickly furred cloak.

"What? What do you understand?"

"Why your cunny is so tight, why you felt like a virgin that first time I entered you."

"I have a child, Gunnar, the queen in case you forget. I was no virgin."

"Aye, I know that, but it has been many year since birth and likely many years since Frode put his cock in you."

"That is true." She paused as the wind howled around the barn and pressed against her. Gunnar held her tighter. "Many years and—"

"And?"

"And he touched me rarely, bedded me rarely, it is the reason I only ever had one child. It was as if he had no interest in laying with me."

"Then the man was a fool, and I am not sure I will feast with him in Valhalla."

"He is no fool, he just...oh, Gunnar, you are the first man who has given me pleasure in ways I could only have dreamed of before."

"That pleases me, woman, of course it does. But I hate to think of your years of frustration."

"Frustration, aye, but you are here now." She touched his cold face. Wiry stubble had sprung on his cheeks and chin. "And I thank all the gods every day that you are here."

"As I thank them for being here." He swept his lips over hers. "Come, let's store this meat then cook and eat. We will have full bellies when we take to our warm bed tonight." He glanced at the longhouse. "And I will worship your body the way it should always have been worshipped."

"I would like that." She smiled, a little fizz of excitement heating between her legs despite the bitter weather.

"You will more than like it, you will cry out my name so loudly, and with such ecstasy that all the gods will hear you. Odin, Thor, Loki, Freya, they will all know how your body reacts to mine and how I can draw such great pulses of pleasure from you."

"Oh, Gunnar, I am so happy you are my man."

"I will always be your Viking man, it is what makes *me* happy."

"What...what are you saying?" Was it what she thought it was? Did he want to wed her?

"That I am your man. No other will ever touch you the way I do. That is what I am saying." He released her suddenly. "Now let us store our meat before the wolves sniff it out." He stooped and filled his arms with the already freezing joints of meat wrapped in linen.

Ingrid stared at his back, as wide as a bear's. He'd brought the conversation to an end, but she wouldn't forget it. Did he want her as his wife? It sounded like it.

She hadn't thought she'd wed again after Frode. She couldn't imagine herself a bride to another man. But that had changed since Gunnar's arrival. She belonged to him now. To be wed, for the people of Halsgrof to know they were wed, she was his, would be a dream come true.

But Gunnar was a Viking explorer. He plied his trade on the high seas, raiding and trading. Would he ever be content to stay here in Cativad or would he leave her for months, years at a time to journey to other lands she could only ever hear about?

'Haps he didn't want to be a husband. 'Haps he just wanted her in his bed each winter. A soft warm body to sink his cock into, to cook his feasts, pour his mead, and naught else.

Would that be enough for her?

Or would she always yearn for more? For the title of wife to Gunnar of Barosvik?

* * *

Ingrid felt beneath her goat's belly. "Good girl, you're going to be a mother, I am sure of it." She smiled as the goat nudged her affectionately. "And you'll take your new babe into the meadow for spring grass, how does that sound?"

The goat bleated, and Ingrid laughed.

Bang. Bang. Bang.

She stood and turned to the barn door. What was Gunnar doing? He'd told her he was clearing snow from the longhouse roof.

Bang. Bang. Bang.

Quickly, she went outside. It was the hour of weak light, and she could see him beside Frode's boat which had been pulled up from the loch before the water had frozen.

Gunnar brought his axe down on it again, smashing the bow clean off.

"What are you doing?" Ingrid shouted, rushing forward.

He raised his head and his arms. The axe blade glinted rose-white. "I am chopping this for firewood."

"But you can't...that is Frode's boat." She had cared for it for years. Had intended to get it repaired in the spring.

"He is long gone." He brought the axe down, splintering the hull further. "And this boat is of no use."

"You can't..." She rushed forward. "You can't destroy it, it belongs to him, it belongs to me."

"What use is a boat full of holes?" He frowned at her. "Do not be dim-witted, woman."

Indignation swarmed within her. Gunnar had no right to destroy her property, nor tell her she was dim-witted. "Do not tell me I am dim-witted, and stop breaking up that boat."

"I will do no such thing." He continued to chop, his thick arm muscles bunching and flexing beneath his tight tunic.

"Gunnar." She stamped her foot. "I told you to stop."

He paused and stared at her, his eyebrows pulled low. "Do not think you can tell me what to do, woman."

"I do not wish that boat to be used as firewood."

"I have decided its fate." He raised the axe. "I will commission a new boat from Halsgrof in the spring."

"But I want *that* boat. I want it repaired."

He crashed the axe down, splintering through the center of the hull this time.

There was no chance the boat could ever be repaired. Not now. And Ingrid knew this. Anger heated her blood, and she swiped at her brow, warm despite the arctic chill. "Stop!" She rushed up to him and grasped his right arm, clung to it.

"Ingrid." He glared down at her. "Release me."

"I want you to leave this boat be."

"Why?" He paused, the axe still and silent. "Because you still love Frode? Wish him here?"

"Frode is feasting with the gods, and he will not be happy that you are destroying his boat."

"I am not considering Frode. I am considering you. Now answer my question."

"I love you," her voice was rising, frustration lacing her words. "I love you, Gunnar, but that does not mean that you can break up this boat. That does not mean you can do what you want around here, I—"

"Which is where you are wrong." His voice was low and husky. "I am the master of this longhouse as you well know."

Of course he was, and he acted that way every day with she, his obedient woman.

Except right now that was annoying her as if she were a serpent who'd had its tail stamped on.

"And as such," he went on, removing her hand from his arm by raising the axe. "I will do as I please and you will accept it."

He dropped the axe, splitting a plank in two.

"I must always just accept what you say? What you do?" she said, and slammed her hands onto her hips.

"Aye, woman, you must." He chopped again. A splinter of wood flew through the air, just missing her shoulder.

She half squealed and half grunted in frustration then stooped and grabbed the slice of sharp wood.

"So return to the longhouse," he said with the axe hoisted above his head. "And make me a meal."

She didn't move. It was as if her boots were full of heavy rocks.

"Now!" he roared. "Before I tip you over my knee for a hard spanking, wench."

His cheeks were flushed; she'd angered him. A spanking was a very real danger.

But he'd angered her, too. His actions, his tone of voice, his threats. It had all made her blood boil and a red mist descended over her vision.

Before she had time to think of consequences, Ingrid hurled the arrow-like piece of wood at him.

It was as if time stood still. It speared through the air on a direct course for his face.

As he dropped the axe down, it sliced against his cheek. By the time it had landed on the ground, a ruby-red gash had appeared on his flesh.

He turned to her, shock and surprise in his eyes, then released the axe by leaving it standing in the wrecked hull.

Without saying a word, he straightened and touched his cheek, dipping his fingertips into the flow of blood. He examined the scarlet tips then turned to her.

"I am sorry," she said, panic replacing her anger. "I am sorry, Gunnar, I didn't mean to—"

"You *meant* to hurt me. You *meant* to take out your wrath on me, on my flesh."

"I didn't think it would... Come to the longhouse, let me clean it for you."

"No. I will clean it myself. But you go to the longhouse, now, and I will deal with you there."

"Deal with me?"

"You have been insolent, your behavior not something I can tolerate or let go unpunished."

"But I am sorry, really, I—"

"Words will not fix this, Ingrid." He pointed at the longhouse. "Now get yourself in there before you earn more swipes to your behind."

Her rump tingled, and she clenched her buttocks. It had been some time since her last spanking. 'Haps she'd forgotten how much she hated it and that was why she'd been brave enough to hurl something at him. Oh, she'd been so foolish. The boat had already been ruined. Why had she made such a fuss?

"The longhouse," he shouted and pointed at it again. "And do not think I will go easy on you, wench."

Chapter Ten

Ingrid rushed to the longhouse. Her breaths were shaky, as were her knees.

No longer thinking about the biting cold, the relentless snow, and the animals, now all her thoughts were on her reckless action and what was going to happen next.

Gunnar was all the more dangerous when he spoke in that deep, rumbling tone—the tone that demanded obedience and dripped with dominance.

And dominate her he would. She was so small and trapped and totally at his mercy. Aye, she wanted to please him, gain words of praise, but the other side of the coin was his wrath, his displeasure when she angered or disappointed him.

Quickly, she set out a clean rag for him to tend his cut, then she walked twice around the fire trough, wringing her hands together. Suddenly hot, she removed her cloak, dropping it to the bench.

Her pulse thudded in her ears, and she wondered if she should bare her bottom ready for him. Would that please him? Save her a few angry spanks?

But before she could do that his bulk shadowed the doorway.

"I have placed a rag there for you, please let me—"

"Do not speak, you have said enough." He stormed in and grabbed the rag. He wiped roughly at his cheek, spreading a smear of blood toward his nose. He then glowered at her as if examining his options. What he should do with her.

'The gods blessed me with imagination when it comes to doling out punishments.'

His words came back to Ingrid, and her belly tightened. There was a different glint in his eye. One that was challenging, confident, perhaps even excited.

Candlelight flickered over his face as he curled his fingers into the neckline of her tunic.

She hitched in a breath, but no sooner had she taken it, it rushed from her lungs.

He'd wrenched the clothing, tearing it clean down her sternum to her belly, the material parting as though butter sliced with a hot knife.

She staggered forward, her balance lost.

He held her tight, righting her in a solid grip.

"Gunnar," she gasped.

"By the time I have finished with you, wench, you will never again speak to me that way, think to tell me what to do, or throw wood at my face."

"I am sorry. I won't do it again."

"I know you won't." Once again, he tore at her tunic. This time it split to the base, exposing her nakedness beneath.

"It is good you don't have undergarments this day." He tossed the tattered tunic to one side. "Now bend over."

She'd expected to go over his lap, but instead he swiped at the table, sending a half-eaten loaf of rye bread and a knife to the floor.

"Oh! But I..." She gasped. He'd doubled her over the cool wood. Her breasts flattened, and her bare bottom rose, vulnerable and quivering.

"Do not move." He set his hand between her shoulders, pinning her in place.

She couldn't move even if she'd wanted to.

Warmth from the fire licked over her right side, Gunnar stood on her left. "Please, not too hard." She reached back and set her hand over her bottom. "I beg you."

"That is not for you to decide." He gripped her forearm and dragged her hand away. "Do not get in my way, you will make this worse for yourself."

The first spank hit fast and sudden.

Ingrid cried out, lunging forward and the table legs scraping.

"I told you to keep still." He increased the pressure on her shoulders. "Keep still and take it."

She gritted her teeth, knowing the next slap was coming swiftly.

It did, landing squarely across both buttocks and sending licks of fire over her skin.

Her cunny tightened, and her bud pulsed. The pain spread between her legs.

"You will never." He spanked her. "Behave this way again." Another spank, then another and another.

Her eyes watered, and she bit on her bottom lip. The searing pain of each slap had barely registered when another layered over it.

The sharp sound of flesh on flesh rang around the longhouse. She was so ashamed of what she'd done, how she'd acted, and as she took her spanking, she knew she'd never throw anything at Gunnar again. "Please...I have learned my lesson." She was panting.

He paused. "You're not even close." He ran his hand over her sore bottom. "And I have barely begun."

"Oh no...I...please." She shifted her hips from left to right.

"Keep still." His palm swiped over her buttocks.

Quickly, he set up a fast spanking rhythm, each one landing with accuracy and delivering stinging heat.

Her cunny dampened. The fire built in her womb, tugging from her a need she didn't understand. She tried to escape it, not wanting to be wanting, and danced on her toes, clawing at the table.

He stopped, his hand squarely on her bottom.

She was burning up, her bottom never so raw and hot as it was now. "Have you finished? Please let that be it, Gunnar, I ask of you, please."

"Stop talking, wench." He stepped away from her. "And do not move."

She was breathing fast, her underarms damp.

He removed his cloak and dropped it beside hers on the chair. He then shoved at his tunic sleeves, pushing them up his arms to expose the roped tendons and muscles beneath his flesh.

She trembled, realizing that he'd spoken the truth, he had barely begun with her.

He walked to the candle box, and when there, paused and stared at her, pinning her to the table with his eyes.

She didn't dare move. She hardly dared breathe.

Apparently satisfied with her obedience, he reached for a long candle about the thickness of three of her fingers. Holding it up, he examined it, ran his fingertip along the length, and nodded.

"What are you—?"

"Did I ask you to speak?"

She shook her head and clamped her lips together. Confusion warred with apprehension. There were candles lit already, they didn't need more.

"Mmm," he said, "this should do."

She knew better than to ask more questions.

Next, he dipped the candle's base in the butter, coating it, then stood behind her.

She peered over her shoulders, the tremble in her belly increasing and the tension in her legs causing them to shake.

"Remember," he said gruffly, "your body is mine, every inch of it, to do as I wish when I wish."

"Aye, Gunnar but..." Her words ran dry. He tugged her smarting left buttock, exposing her anus.

In that moment, she realized his plan. "Oh, no...you can't...I..."

She tried to push from the table, escape, but his hand slapped onto her shoulders, imprisoning her against the wood. "You will take this candle where I choose to put it."

"Oh, but really...not there."

"Aye, there." He touched the buttered end to the center of her hole.

Instinctively, she clenched. No man had ever touched her rear hole before. And now Gunnar wanted to put that in it…it was unthinkable.

"You will make this worse for yourself if you fight me." He increased the pressure, and her delicate, slippery hole was opened. "Let it in, Ingrid, let it inside you." His voice was soothing, encouraging, as though he was being kindly to her. "Do not oppose your punishment, one you brought entirely upon yourself."

She didn't think his tone would last. Her crime was too great, and he was right, she had brought it on herself.

Staring straight ahead at the furs laid on the bed, she held her breath. The candle was actually sliding into her bottom now. Her tight pucker had parted around it, and the smooth invasion wasn't nearly as unpleasant as she'd thought it might be.

He continued to penetrate her. His action so dark, so crude, yet oh so intimate.

Again she warred with herself, a battle of knowing this was her punishment and designed to humiliate and pain her, yet at the same time finding the candle slipping into her an erotic new sensation that didn't hurt in the slightest.

"You have taken it," he said. "And it will remain there until I decide to remove it."

"Aye…aye, I understand."

"Now to resume the spanking." He slapped her right cheek.

"Oh, but how…ouch!" It was impossible not to clamp around the candle as the heat of the spank shot over her skin.

He spanked her again, her left cheek this time.

Again she gripped the candle. It shifted inside her, and she groaned, a low, rattling moan.

"I see this punishment is working," he said. "You are learning a lesson you will never forget."

"I won't…forget," she managed. "Oh!"

He was spanking her, taking it in turns to swipe each buttock. Once more, the heat was growing, and the sharp sting of his palm stacking up the burn. He moved lower, to the tops of her thighs, and she cried out, the pain here new and sharp.

"Be quiet," he said. "Take it with dignity."

It was hard to feel dignified with a candle up her anus and her bottom being reddened by a big brute of a Viking. She cried out again and squeezed her buttocks together. The candle moved.

"Stop that," he snapped. "Keep still. Keep quiet."

She sniffed, her nose running now. "Please, no more, it pains me so. I will be good, I promise."

"Your self-control is severely lacking, woman, and I am about to remedy that." He stepped away, to the fire, and took a long matchwood. He lit it, then held it up.

"What...what are you doing?" She twisted to see him.

"I am going to light the candle protruding from your little bottom hole, and you will not move. If you do, it will drip hot wax onto your legs." He touched the match to the wick. A happy little orange flame sprang to life. "Keep still." He blew the matchwood out. "For if you burn yourself with hot wax that will also displease me."

"I...I'll try."

"Aye, you will." He stroked her bottom as if examining his red handiwork and the imprints of his fingers.

She held herself still. A drip of arousal had slicked from her cunny to her inner thighs. Would he discover it? Would he harshen her punishment if he knew her need to feel his cock sinking deep was growing with each breath she took?

"Oh, Gunnar..." she moaned.

"I told you to be quiet." He walked around the table, his footsteps heavy thumps. "Yet you do not appear to be capable of that."

"I am sorry, Gunnar, but oh..." A ray of heat from the lit candle in her bottom blossomed over her flesh. She really did have to keep still. So still.

"Still talking, huh." He grunted and removed his buckled belt. It fell to the floor with a clang. "I can soon stop that."

He shoved his pants down his legs until they sat around his hairy thighs. He took his erect cock in his fist.

She stared at it, so close to her face she could see every vein. The end was wide and glossy, the slit deep.

"Open your mouth." He gripped a handful of her hair, holding her head up, her face angled at his cock. "Open up and take me. Use your teeth and you will have tripled your punishment tonight."

"Gunnar..." He was going to fill her mouth with his cock. He'd never done that before. She really had annoyed him with her talking.

"Do it. Open." He tugged her hair roots.

She did as he'd asked, stretching her mouth wide.

His cock was instantly there, slipping between her lips and onto her tongue.

He was hot and hard, musky and dark, and as he slid deeper, she breathed in absorbing his scent as well as his taste.

"Aye, your sweet mouth," he said on a groan. "Keep taking me. Keep taking me."

Ingrid didn't have much choice. The candle protruding from her bottom continued to burn, and her mouth was filled with her Viking master's thick cock.

He moaned as if he were already feasting in Valhalla. "Ah...good...good."

She hugged his hot shaft with her tongue.

He grunted and slid in deeper.

Her mouth was so full of him, her cheeks bulging, her throat butted up against.

Just when she feared he might go too deep, he withdrew to her lips, giving her time to snatch a breath, then he slipped in again.

His hold on her hair was rigid as he filled her then pulled back. He treated her mouth the way he did her cunny, in and out, working his cock into her over and over.

Her stomach was tense with excitement. Would he spill his seed into her throat?

More arousal leaked from her cunny. She was totally at his mercy, a plaything, a disobedient wench who needed teaching a lesson.

She was hot and breathless now, her hole quivering around the candle.

"You have a good mouth," he said, swinging his hips. He was using her for his own pleasure. "Like that, aye, with your tongue."

She continued to wrap her tongue around his cock, holding it tight.

Again he moaned, and this time he also sent thanks to the gods above.

Heat from the candle's flame flickered on her thighs. She knew it wouldn't have burned down yet but she craved a look at it, to see, to check.

"I know what you are thinking," he said. "The candle is still long; do not fear, when I have finished with your mouth, I will attend to it."

She couldn't answer, her mouth was stuffed full of cock. A brief image of what she must look like popped into her head. What Frode would think if he could see what was happening in the longhouse he'd built with his own hands.

A wash of shame crept over her. She'd allowed Gunnar to own her, to take her any way he wanted to. She didn't fight his strength, his dominance, but then what would be the point?

Frode would never have treated her this way—spanked her, breached her bottom, treated her mouth like a cunny.

But she loved Gunnar. She wanted to please him. To be his obedient woman...his obedient wife.

"Ah, my love, you are going to make me spill my seed too soon." Suddenly, he pulled out of her mouth and released her hair. "You are very skilled at that."

She was breathing fast, her lips puffy and her mouth empty.

He stepped away and gripped his cock. "I should check the candle sticking from your rear, don't you think?"

"Aye." Her bottom trembled. The skin was still tingling from the spanking, as though a nest of red ants had taken a fancy to it. Her hole clamped and released; she was sure that would move the candle.

"It is burning bright," he said. "It has some time to go, but you have done well, the wax has not spilled to your legs."

"I have tried to be still."

"You did well." He was stroking her bottom, then the top of her left leg, then between her thighs. "Oh, Ingrid...what have I found?"

Chapter Eleven

Ingrid gulped as Gunnar scooped his fingers through her wet swollen folds to her entrance.

"You are wet and ready for cock. Your cunny is so greedy and demanding, even when you are being punished for bad behavior, being spanked for throwing things at me and cutting me."

"I...I am sorry."

"A cunny this badly behaved doesn't deserve cock," he said. "What do you think?"

"I...I wish to please you, Gunnar, whatever you wish is what I wish."

He laughed, a strange tight noise that came from his throat. "In that case, I will take exactly what I want."

"Which is?"

"Which is something you are about to find out." He blew on the candle, extinguishing the flame, then stood directly behind her. He set one hand over her right buttock as if to ensure she didn't move.

And then the candle was being withdrawn. Slowly, oh so slowly, he took it out of her bottom. Her small hole was aware of its smoothness, its length, and then it clattered to the floor.

"This is what I wish for," he said, splaying his fingers roughly through her cunny then rubbing her sweet spot in hard, fast circles.

She moaned and rested her forehead on the table. "Gunnar."

"I will coat my cock with your wetness," he said. "And then..."

"And then...oh..."

His cock was at her entrance. He pushed in, filling her in one smooth glide.

"Oh, in the name of all the gods." She took him and ground her swelling bud on the lip of the table. "Aye, like that."

He placed his free hand on her other cheek and used his fingers like pincers on her raw rump.

She cried out, and her heart rate sped up. She'd soon be able to claim pleasure if he worked her like this, from behind. It would be so good.

But then he withdrew. His cock left her cunny and didn't push back in on an urgent curl of his hips the way she was expecting.

She arched her back and shifted her hips, searching for him, wanting to seek pleasure now her spanking had ended.

"Do not forget your place," he said gruffly. "You are under me, tipped over for my pleasure, not yours. I am reminding you of your position. I am taking what is mine, what I possess, what I own."

Desire shot around her body. She wanted him to fill her with his cock, his seed, take her with him as he found his angry, possessive release.

"Keep still, wench, this will be uncomfortable, shocking even, but it will happen...now."

The smooth dome of his cock was suddenly pressed up against her rear hole.

"Gunnar!" She tried to twist, to shove away, but didn't move an inch. He had a tight hold of her by her buttocks. "Oh, for the love of Odin, what are you doing?"

"You know what I am doing, I have prepared you, now relax and take my big Viking cock into your naughty little bottom."

Her mouth hung open as he increased the pressure. He really thought his cock would fit in there? He was so big, so hard, so thick.

Her hole could not fight against him. He held her securely and spread her tight ring of muscle over his glans.

"In the name of..." he gasped. "You should see yourself like this, taking my cock."

Ingrid could only imagine, and she groaned as her pucker was stretched wider, wider still. He wasn't going fast, he was savoring each tiny entry.

On and on he went. Her ring of muscle expanding.

"Oh!" She panted through a slice of pain, and then he was in.

"Ah, sweet bottom, your sweet bottom," he said, his grip on her sore buttocks clamping harder. "This will not be the last time I take you here. You are so tight, a virginal hole."

He let out a low, primitive growl and sank deep, filling her with a dark density that had her cunny weeping and her bud engorging. He kept on going until his balls pressed up against her wetness.

"Ah, my woman." He released her buttocks and leaned forward, his chest on her back, his mouth by her ear. "Say you are mine."

"Aye, aye, I am yours." She was breathless and filled absolutely. This man in her, and over her, was her world, her day and night, her every breath.

"Say it again."

"Yours. I am yours."

He pumped his hips, small movements that slid his cock a little way out then deep into her bottom.

Each time he hit full depth her swollen bud rubbed on the table. She moaned. The pressure grew. The weight of his cock in her was so dense, so heavy.

"You are mine," he said gruffly, his breaths hot on the shell of her ear. "No one else will ever have you. You are mine. For all of time. Mine. Mine. Mine." He punctuated the last three words with deeper, harder thrusts, his body hair rubbing on the tormented flesh on her rump.

"Oh, more..." Ingrid had barely had time to think about how amazing it felt to have him in her bottom because her orgasm was racing toward her. "More."

"Do not order me, wench, or I will withdraw and leaving you wanting."

She bit on her bottom lip, willing herself to stop speaking, even though she wanted to cry out her desire for him and demand that her satisfaction be delivered.

He continued to claim her, his cock thick and unrelenting.

She closed her eyes as the pressure grew. Her release was going to be spectacular and deep, and she feared her heart might not survive the intensity.

And then it was there. He'd worked so far into her, and her cunny could hold off no longer.

"Ah! Gunnar! I'm..." Pleasure exploded. Her hole squeezed his cock root over and over, waves of bliss that spread around her body.

He set his teeth on the fleshy part of her earlobe, his breaths a storm as he, too, let his pleasure release.

He shook with her. He gasped with her. She had never known anything like it. Her entire pelvis was being ravaged by wild spasms, and each one shot bliss to her cunny, her rear hole, and then around her body.

He was groaning with his fingers curled around the head end of the table, holding on to it so tightly his knuckles had whitened.

She was aware of his cock throbbing. The primitive sounds erupting from his throat and rattling from his chest to her shoulders sent new highs of ecstasy through her. They were one. Man and woman. She had never felt so safe, so satisfied, so utterly owned and protected.

"My woman," he said breathily. "You will learn to obey me at all times, it is how I will ensure your happiness and safety."

"Aye. Oh, Gunnar, aye, I promise to do better." Her breaths were hard to catch. "I will make you proud."

"I know you will." He kissed her cheek, then gripped her hair, turning her head so he could capture her lips.

Their tongues slicked together. His cock slicked in and out of her hole. A gentle glide as he softened.

Eventually their breaths steadied, and he pulled out, his hot chest leaving her back when he straightened.

Ingrid was dizzy, exhausted, spent, her flesh damp and her buttocks sore. A shake started in her knees and went upward, to her thighs, her cunny, belly, then the length of her spine. Her teeth clattered, and her shoulders shook.

"Hey, woman, I've got you." He threw a thick fur rug over her body.

Still she shook. It was uncontrollable.

And then his arms were around her, and he was scooping her up and off the table. Holding her close.

He embraced her with strength and moved to the chair beside the fire. Sitting, he set her on his lap with her face in the groove of his neck.

She inhaled his scent. A full-body tremble attacked her. It was as if every part of her was being rattled.

"Shh." He stroked her hair back from her brow. "I've got you."

"What...what is happening to me?"

"You've had an intense experience, your body is reacting as though it has been in battle."

"Battle?"

He kissed the top of her head and held her tight in his embrace. "Aye, it is to be expected after pain and pleasure. Soon it will pass."

She closed her eyes and tried to ignore the pins of hurt on her buttocks. He'd been right when he'd said she wouldn't sit comfortably for a week. Her bottom had been thoroughly punished by his hand.

But the rest of her, that didn't hurt. Satisfaction lay on her the way the fur was. It wrapped around her the way Gunnar's arms were. Her heart still thudded, each beat laced with contentment.

She sighed.

"That's it, relax." His voice was low and gentle. "I will not let you go, I will hold you together until you can hold yourself together again."

Ingrid didn't know how Gunnar had gotten so wise about such things. 'Haps it was from many years of raiding and battles. 'Haps it was Viking instinct. But that didn't matter, she knew he would hold her until she felt stronger. She trusted him to be there, always.

* * * *

There were times in the past Winterfest had slipped by without a traditional festival. There simply hadn't been enough food to feast upon.

But this year with Gunnar's hunting and trapping skills, plus the supplies sent from Queen Tove and King Njal, Ingrid was excited to mark the passing of the shortest day of the winter.

It would be many weeks until the sun peeked above the horizon, a brief greeting to start with, but the slice of heat and light would grow until eventually the full golden orb would grace the spring sky once again.

Plants would grow, animals would graze, and the furs, blankets, and rugs would be cleaned and left to dry in a pleasant, grass-scented breeze. Ingrid longed for summer months, for dips in the loch, and wide blue skies.

"Skål," Gunnar said, raising a horn of mead. "To our feast of Winterfest."

"Skål." Ingrid lifted her glass of buttermilk. Lately, she'd gone off the taste of mead.

"The deer smells good." He stirred the broth. "I will get you a bowl."

"No, I can do that." She set her buttermilk aside and stood. "Oh!"

"What is it?" He turned to her with a frown.

"I just…" She rubbed her temple. "A little dizzy."

"Why is that so?"

"Tired." She gestured to the table laden with freshly baked rye, piles of pickles, shelled nuts, and cabbage. "It has been a busy day."

"The animals tire you? Caring for them?"

"No, I like to care for them. We will have newly borns in the spring. Both of the young goats are pregnant, the ram you brought has done his job."

"That is good." He gestured to her chair. "Sit."

"No I can serve, it is my duty."

"It is also your duty to obey me, now sit, wench, before I spank you."

Ingrid sat. She was thankful now that her bottom no longer pained her from her last spanking, it had been nearly seven nights since Gunnar had tipped her over the very table their feast now lay on and put a candle, then his cock in her rear hole.

"Here." He handed her a bowl of steaming broth. "Eat, you need your strength in winter, and it has pleased me to see meat coming to your bones. When I arrived you were so frail."

"Aye, it is good to have food." Though as she looked at her meal, her stomach rolled.

Gunnar shoveled his broth into his mouth using a large whalebone spoon. "Mmm, it is good." He nodded at her. "Eat."

"'Haps later." She set the bowl aside.

"Ingrid." He stared at her, his spoon halfway to his mouth. "You are concerning me."

"There is no need to be concerned." She shrugged. "Tired, that is all."

He set his food on the table and stood. He walked around the fire trough, his frown deepening. "It is Winterfest, am I right?"

"Of course you are right, we are feasting."

"And I arrived at the first snow, two full moons ago, longer 'haps."

"Aye." She watched him staring into space, and a slew of realizations tumbled into her. Suddenly, she knew what he was thinking, she knew the notion that had emerged in his mind.

For two full moons he had been emptying his seed into her, keeping them both warm and satisfied on the coldest of days.

And now, like the goats, she was with child.

Child!

A babe. Again. Her? It was a wonderful thought that instantly brought sunshine to her heart. Could she be so lucky? Had the gods designed her fate that she should carry Gunnar of Barosvik's child, his son, a strong Viking warrior son?

"Gunnar," she said quietly.

He turned and raked his hand over his stubbled jawline. "Aye."

"For two moons now, I haven't…"

"Go on." His brow creased.

"I haven't bled."

"And you would expect to?"

"Of course."

He didn't speak. His nostrils flared as he took a deep breath.

She set her hand on her belly. "I am," she said softly, "with child."

He nodded. One fast up-down of his head. "Aye, I believe that is so."

She swallowed. Was he pleased? What would she do if he wasn't?

He came closer, then squatted before her, placed his hands on her knees. "My child. My first child." He paused, emotion flashing in his eyes. "And I know you will be a fine mother to my son. Caring and nurturing, strong yet soft."

"I will try my best."

"You have already raised a queen, my woman, you will also raise a warrior. I know that, the way I know my heart loves you."

Her eyes prickled, tears of happiness forming. "I love you, too."

Gunnar leaned forward and moved her hand from her belly. He kissed her through her clothing, in the exact spot she believed their babe to be growing. His eyes fluttered closed.

Ingrid touched his plaited hair and wondered what he was seeing in his future. A babe in his arms? A son to build a boat with? Or a warrior to raid and battle with, a man he could and would defend with his life?

"We will raise the child here," he said. "And ensure he learns the ways of the land. To hunt and trap, to build a home and boats, to understand the seasons and the animals that share the mountains and lochs with us."

"But what about your travels?"

He paused then. "I have traveled for many years. Maybe the gods have sent me this gift to tame my wandering ways."

"You want to stay here, live here for all of our mortal lives?"

"Aye, we will make this farm a success. We will have a family."

She nodded. "Can I ask one thing?"

"Aye, of course." He stroked her belly, the warmth of his hand spreading to her skin.

She studied the shadows dancing on his face. "Can we still go to Halsgrof to see Queen Tove in the spring?"

"That would be for the best."

"It would?"

"Aye." He downturned his mouth. "For I have little experience in childbirth, it is best for you to have women helping you."

She smiled. "That is a truth."

He stood and gently pulled her with him. He held her close with his arms wrapped around her. "When I was given the task of delivering supplies to Cativad by King Njal, I was not happy. After months of journeying, all I wanted was to sup mead with warriors and discuss our travels, plan our next raids but..."

"But?"

His eyes bored into her. "The task has proven to be one of the most important in my life. It was as if the king had spoken directly to the gods and they had planned our meeting, Ingrid, our winter together."

"Oh, Gunnar." Ingrid's heart swelled with love. "When you beat on my door that night my life changed, my world changed, and now I can't imagine you not being in it, at my side. I am so proud to be carrying your child. I will not let you down."

"I know you won't, wife."

"Wife?"

He chuckled. "It is only right we be wed upon our arrival at Halsgrof."

"You wish me to be your bride?"

"If you wish me to be your husband." He raised his eyebrows.

"Aye. Oh, more than anything else on this earth, that is what I wish."

Ingrid felt as though she were flying in the clouds, an eagle high on happiness. For the first time in so many years her future was bright and warm. With Gunnar at her side, it would be an eternal summer, and she was to become a mother and a wife again, wishes she hadn't even dared to entertain.

The gods had been kind to her, 'haps they'd forgotten that she'd existed. She had been so quiet living alone with Tove by the loch. But they had only forgotten her for a while. Because then they'd sent a strong, wise warrior who loved her and whom she loved in return.

"Then it is settled." Gunnar dipped his head. "We will be man and wife." He pressed his lips over hers. A wonderful deep kiss that sealed their future together in this life and the next. Theirs was a bond that could not be broken.

THE END

ABOUT THE AUTHOR

Lily Harlem is an award-winning, bestselling author of sexy romance. She writes in many genres and pairings so there is plenty to choose from on her website.

SUBMITTING TO THE VIKING WARRIOR is a spin-off novel from MASTERED BY THE VIKING KING so don't miss out on meeting Ingrid's daughter Tove and her masterful new royal husband, King Njal.

Find out more on Lily's website - www.lilyharlem.com